I0522572

The Ethereal Transit Society

Thomas Vaughn

Printed in the United States of America
First Edition: 2020
eBook ISBN 978-1-7355829-0-0
Softcover ISBN 978-0-9960381-9-5

Published By Bad Dream Entertainment®
www.BadDreamEntertainment.com

Cover Illustration and Design by Victoria Lester
Final Manuscript Polish by Melissa Peitsch

The 'EyeBrain' logo is a registered trademark of Bad Dream Entertainment, Seattle, WA.
Original trademark design by Darcray

For Valerie

I always make it a priority to check out the shithouse prophets when I find myself in a new place. It seems like the worse the town is, the more profound their insights. I scan the graffiti on the bathroom stall, filtering out the scatological limericks and requests for ten-inch dicks. The piss vapors sting my eyes. The racist epitaphs remind me I'm in the South—way out in the sticks. Then I see what I'm looking for. The prophecy takes the form of a Eucharistic call and response.

What will we do with all of these little brown babys?

The misspelled question is scrawled in black magic marker. Right below, in a steadier hand, comes the riposte.

We will baptise them in the waters of death before they drink the blood of our daugters.

"Amen, brothers," I chuckle. We're in the right place. There's no doubt about that. Something has these hillbillies on edge. They're scared and they don't know why. Even after Quint's death he still has the ability to freak people out. But that's the way it is with a good messiah. They just won't stay dead and buried.

I step gingerly toward the sink, avoiding the pile of soiled toilet paper on the floor. These roadside shit-stops are never big on hygiene. I twist the knob on the sink and admire the modest trickle of water that issues from the lime-encrusted faucet.

"This sure as hell ain't Malibu," I say, my voice echoing off the stained ceiling tiles. "We're a long way from home."

When I turn to the leave the restroom I'm careful to adjust the mask I wear over the right side of my head. I don't want to make the locals more nervous than they already are.

Only about half the store's shelves are stocked. There are three kinds of beer and only two brands of soda. I'm due for another Oxy so I look around for something to put in my stomach. There's some unsavory fried catfish lying fallow in a grease-stained warmer. The edges are dry and curled. One corner of the store is dedicated to 'live bait,' and most of the minnows in the algae-covered tank are dead. Overhead, the florescent lights flicker on and off.

If the end of the world happened, I'm not sure anyone around here would notice much of a difference.

I select some packaged chips and haul myself to

the counter where a young girl watches me with lazy curiosity. She looks about eighteen. I detect the edge of a tribal tattoo peeking out from the gap between her shirt and jeans.

"This it?" she asks, her eyes avoiding mine when she sees the mask covering half my face.

"This will do it. That is, unless you have some organic Gouda." I smile to put her at ease, but then I remember that doesn't work anymore. My smile just agitates people these days.

"You folks from California?"

"That's right. How did you know?"

"I heard you talking to yourself in the restroom. I wasn't trying to listen or nothin', but your voice kind of carries."

"That it does. This is the first time me and my friends have visited Arkansas."

"I figured. What brings you way out here? You don't seem like the kind of guy who'd hunt."

"We're just humble pilgrims making our holy trek to Mecca."

She looks puzzled, then sighs. "There ain't no place like that around here."

The store is on a one-lane county road and I never thought such a desolate place could exist. The thought of the girl wasting her youth amid the half-empty shelves saddens me. These verdant mountains imprison her just as surely as any cage.

"Looks like you don't have a lot of stock right now."

"It's been slow ever since the trouble last fall, now all we see is local trade. The past few months have been pretty bad for business. Losing the hunters was rough."

"What's up with the hunters? These hills are beautiful. They must be teeming with game."

"The animals have been kind of scarce lately. Then there was the killings. Three hunters got shot last season. Two died."

"No shit? What happened?"

"Nothing, just got themselves shot was all."

"By the same guy?"

"No. They was all accidents. At least that's what people say." She stares through the windows into the sun-drenched afternoon and I remember the words on the bathroom stall. Then she says, more to herself than to me, "Seems like no one really likes going back in those hills now."

I get my stuff and turn to leave.

"Hey!" she calls after me. "How come you wear that mask?"

I glance over my shoulder with my one good eye.

"Because last year I shot half my face off."

I laugh.

Her face clouds.

"I was having a bad week," I add by way of explanation, then laugh again.

It's like that when I'm in performance mode. Always laughing. Particularly when I'm not supposed to.

The stifling July air greets me like a hammer when I exit the store. A crow picks at some flattened roadkill next to the lone gas pump. The town is called Crossroads, though I use the term *town* loosely. Along with the gas station there is a church, a pawn shop, and a scrapyard. That's about it. The others are already in the SUV.

"You teasing the local wildlife?" asks Danielle when I open the door and squeeze into the passenger seat. Xi is sitting in the back, studying her phone.

"I was just talking to that girl in there. You know they had three hunting accidents up here last fall. That's weird."

"Not really. You get a bunch of drunk rednecks together all decked out in camouflage and of course they start shooting each other. It's Mother Earth's way of cleansing herself. By the way, while you were wasting time, Xi and I had to sit here while that guy leered at us."

I look over my shoulder and see a gaunt man leaning against a rusted pick-up truck with rotting wood panels. He wears soiled clothes and a stained cap on his head. His eyes seem haunted.

"What does he want?"

Danielle looks at me like I'm stupid. "Oh, I don't know, Simon." Her voice drips with sarcasm. "How many black people have you seen out here so far? He's probably trying to decide whether or not to tie me to his back bumper and drag me to his favorite lynching tree. And it's not like you and Xi really blend in either."

I study the man. He looks as if he's lost in some painful meditation. "I don't think so. The guy looks scared to me. You want me to go talk to him?"

"Jesus! No! You're just clueless. Why do you always have to talk to strangers? It's your fault we're in this godforsaken hole in the first place."

It's been like this since crossing the Madison County line.

"I didn't ask you to come out here," I say by way of defense.

"No. But it was your lack of faith that stranded us here. If you just hadn't been so…weak."

The last word hovers between us like a poisonous insect.

"If my readings are correct, we should be eight point three kilometers from the turn-off."

Xi delivers the intervention with clipped precision as she taps the map on her phone. High cheek bones contrast with her plain, boyish haircut. She still wears the matching black outfit with the red insignia at her breast. "If we wish to avoid unwanted attention from the indigenous life forms, I suggest we initiate departure."

That's Xi, Vulcan to the core.

I study the man watching us. He's unshaven and his hair drips just over his shirt collar. I notice a scar on his left cheek. His appearance reminds me of a coyote, sleek and half-starved.

"There's some weird shit going on around here," I mutter to myself.

"Give it a break. You're always saying that. We've all got eyes and ears; there's nothing special about this place or your powers of perception."

This time I rise to Danielle's goading. "Maybe you're the one who should give it a break. No one asked you to save me…"

My voice trails away when I realize what I've said. Danielle glares at me.

"Someone *did* ask us. *He* asked us. Xi and I would have made the Transit if we hadn't been chasing after you. So don't pretend this isn't your fault; it's one hundred percent your fault."

A year ago, the press referred to the three of us as the 'survivors'. That's not entirely accurate. You might call us the left-behinds. We were part of a group called the Ethereal Transit Society, though eventually we dropped the *society* bit. People up and down the coast knew us as Ethereal Transit, or ET for short. Quint was a visionary—his name a shortened version of Quintessence, the perfected matter that provides coherence to the universe. He was the greatest man I've ever known, and when he needed me most, I let him down.

While I sat in a Van Nuys motel, crying like a baby with a pistol shoved in my mouth, thirty-five of my colleagues were departing Outpost Earth permanently. The morphine had dulled their senses, followed by a healthy dose of midazolam—a benzodiazepine given to patients undergoing intubation. It basically tells your body to stop struggling for breath. I don't know why he picked Danielle and Xi to follow me. Maybe Xi was selected because of that paramedic training in her pre-awakened life. She once demonstrated her skill during a tuning session after this guy freaked out and put his head through a window. I can still remember the way she stitched the wound with expert calm.

I've never known her pre-awakened name. To us, she's always been Xi.

But sending a protégé like Danielle riding to my rescue? Who can fathom the mind of a messiah?

I stare at the floorboard, lost for a moment in my own self-disgust. She's right. If it wasn't for me, the two of them wouldn't be here.

"This coffee is terrible," Danielle says bitterly, then starts the engine and pulls back onto the lonely county road. The crow looks up from its meal, watching us depart with dull indifference. And, once again, we push into the shimmering heat that threatens to combust the desiccated brush in the hills around us. If planet Earth has an asshole, this is it.

~

You're not looking in the right place. Do you see where my thumb is?

It still gives me pleasure to remember the night Quint showed me the Transit Light. I was a twenty-something dropout tending bar in an L.A. dive when he walked in wearing those black pajamas and red slippers. We saw some strange people in there, but somehow they all fit together. The homeless people, artists, hustlers, and nobodies were part of the desperate pastiche of the city. L.A. was just one blasted mosaic of grotesque wealth juxtaposed with deprivation. And there I was in the middle of it, trying to sell a screenplay about a guy trying to sell a screenplay.

But *he* stood out. Even in all that weirdness, with his shaved head and almond brown eyes, he drew sideways glances. I will never forget the way he paused at the entrance to the bar for a few seconds, haloed by the setting sun, the concert fliers wafting in the ocean breeze. He seemed to be scanning the room, as if looking for a missing child, before walking up to the bar. That is to say, he walked toward me. He wasn't looking for a drink. That's how it was with him; he could make you feel like you were the only person in the universe. There was this calm smile on his face and everything about him exuded equanimity. When he spoke, there was no trace of dialect. In all the years I knew him, he never talked about his childhood.

"What can I get for you, bro?" I asked.

"Do you really feel like you belong here?" he replied in a rich tenor.

The dude radiated power. It was like he was

looking right into me. I couldn't speak at first.

"You only have a short time," he continued. "Do you really want to spend it here, Simon?"

How the fuck had he known my name?

"It's all I've got, man." I felt a deep well of sadness inside me.

"You deserve more. If you're willing, I can show you something that will change your life. I can show you the Transit Light. Only a few are chosen, my friend. You don't belong here any more than a human belongs in a zoo. It's time for you to wake up."

That night I found myself on the pier with the peripatetic guru, watching the planes crisscross a sea of stars. He told me about the ship that was coming to rescue him and a few select others. I never went in for that UFO shit, but I tolerated the line because there was something inside of me that was hungry. I was teetering on the edge of oblivion and needed meaning. When he put his hand on my shoulder, it felt like I had just been plugged into a battery charger. It wasn't like speed, it was pure and beautiful. I looked down the length of his extended arm, focusing on that point in the sky above his thumb. Then I noticed one light was a little different from the others. It was undulating back and forth.

"That's weird," I said, now deeply engrossed.

"You see it! Good! Most people cannot *see*. I knew you had the capacity for vision the moment I saw you, Simon."

We watched the orb hovering for about a half hour. Neither of us said a word. Then it suddenly shifted direction and dodged below the horizon.

"And there it goes," he said sadly. "It's studying us. But one day it will come. No one can tell when that day will happen, but it approaches just as sure as death. It will sweep us up. The planet will be recycled in a great cataclysm. Our vehicles will be left behind like broken husks. The chosen ones will watch from afar, our bodies remolded into pure energy. Will you come with me, Simon? Will you join me on this great adventure?"

Fuck yeah.

After that night, things seemed so clear. Everything had its purpose and place. It was a powerful transition. In my pre-awakened life, I was just another bland face in the crowd, struggling to survive. Then, out of the blue, this holy man extended the hand of salvation. Sometimes I would give anything to go back there.

I don't spend much time watching the sky these days. It's just one big canopy of darkness.

~

"Christ!" shouts Danielle when the SUV hits another pothole, rattling the length of its frame. "Don't they have maintenance out here?"

She has a point. I've never seen roads this shitty. We've been driving for at least three miles since leaving the highway and already missed two turns. The road is lined by barbed-wire fence on either side. Occasionally, a lazy cow pokes its head through a gap. The road rises and falls as we pass shacks and trailers teetering on the edge of steep hillsides. Trash and cast-off appliances are piled in yards where sun-stroked dogs lay panting. Occasional driveways snake off from either side of the road. Rarely do we see a single mailbox—usually there are at least four or five, indicating that an entire clan shares a small piece of property dotted with campers and rusted satellite dishes.

For all the signs of sporadic human activity, I don't see a single person. At least these rednecks are smart enough to stay inside when the sun is out. I thought I had felt heat before, but never anything like this. It sucks the guts right out you—makes you a coward. I still can't believe Quint spent his childhood here. He was so full of life. Everything in this place is either dead or dying. It's a hungry land.

Even the vines seem determined to strangle the life from the spindly trees.

"Man, it's sad how poor these people are. It makes me think about that girl stuck back in that store. I wonder if she lives in one of these places."

We saw our share of poverty in California. Most of it was transient. You got used to homeless people lying outside multi-million-dollar mansions. But there's nothing in this place. These people have grown up out the black soil, generations of them living like trash pickers for a hundred years. They stick to the sides of these mountains like rotting fungi, forced to bear witness to the slow debilitation of the seasons.

"Who would ever had figured Quint grew up in a place like this?"

"Nobody said he grew up here," Danielle snaps.

"Why else would he have his body shipped all the way out here? You think he just threw a dart at a map?"

She grows silent, a quiet confession that I'm probably right.

After the coroner pulled the others out of the Malibu pad in body bags, it turned out Quint was the only one who had made burial arrangements. How about that for a punch in the gut? A few of our people had family claim them, but the majority of ET's crew members were cremated and then unceremoniously dumped in a mass grave at L.A. County Cemetery. Xi told us workers in hazmat suits just emptied one zip-lock bag after another into the hole while a bored-looking guy sat chain-smoking in an idling backhoe, waiting for the signal to fill in the grave and put the whole fucked-up episode to rest.

Man, how people love to bury their problems.

"Just another bunch of dead, suicidal nuts," opined one radio host.

It only took the reporters one day to locate me in the hospital. They came by the dozens, asking for lurid details of sexual debauchery. The fact was, most of us were celibate. There wasn't anything strange about it. Nobody gave a shit about sex because we were on the cusp of a new age in human history. We were going places. The body is nothing but a vessel for housing the awareness. There's no way to explain an idea like that to an outsider. They could never understand the desire to plug into the cosmic ether that held the universe together. We were training ourselves to be masters of energy and matter. That's what the tuning sessions were all about.

The DA was a total bitch. There I was with half

my face missing and all she could think about was pinning the whole thing on me. I didn't rat on Danielle or Xi. They both went underground, leaving me to face the wolves. It's hard for the unawakened to fathom that thirty-five bodies could turn up in a posh Malibu neighborhood without a crime having been committed. Hell, it was possibly the most beautiful moment in human history and all they could do was look for scapegoats. In the end, the cops lost interest about the same time the press did.

Funny how that happens.

As the vehicle tilts precariously across a rutted lane I reach up and probe my face. The bullet hadn't gone straight through my frontal lobe — the part of the brain housing all the higher reasoning functions — as I'd intended. I wanted to kill my awareness. It started the night Quint showed me what the next level was going to look like — what was getting ready to go down. I couldn't handle it. It still puzzles me that I was the one he confided in. Why not Danielle? She was the strong one.

"You shouldn't take so many of those things," she says, twisting the wheel from side to side, trying to keep the vehicle on the road. She watches me fingering the Oxy bottle in my pocket. It turns out my palate had been thicker than normal—or at least that's what the doctor said. The 9mm round deviated through my upper molars, carving a channel through the cheek bone and eye socket. That meant the right side of my face was a puckered mess, even with the titanium plate. But one of the few perks of having half a face is that the doctors don't argue with you about your pain dosage.

"They get me through the day," I reply, watching as we pass by a limestone cliff jutting from the leaf clutter. A single tree grows from a crack in its face, determined to survive in the face of implacable hostility.

"You're obstructing your higher source."

"I haven't felt the higher source in a long time."

"That's not true and you know it. You perceived the signal just like us. If you just used the pain mantra correctly, you wouldn't need those pills."

Just as I am about to argue, Xi interrupts.

"Astra, I'm getting some strange readings here." She holds her phone at face level, lips pursed.

Xi never uses our pre-awakened names.

"What is it?" Danielle asks.

"The signal has been compromised."

"You told me this place was covered by the network."

"I don't think that is the problem."

Danielle abruptly pulls off to the side of the road so she can give the situation her full attention. When I turn to the backseat, I see the puzzled look on Xi's face. She has angular features, accentuated by thick eyebrows. There is a faint smile on her face. That's rare.

"What's up, Xi? Have the groundhogs uprooted the cell tower?" I ask.

"I don't think so," she replies, affecting a slight Scottish accent. She does this from time to time when something amuses her. "I believe that Quint has infiltrated the signal."

"What the fuck are you talking about?" It would be easy to mistake Xi's eccentricities for mental instability. Nothing could be further from the truth. She's a little younger than Danielle and me, but not given to hyperbole. Xi is straight-shit, high-functioning. "What does Quint have to do with the cellphone?"

Slowly she turns the screen toward us. It's black except for a bright light in the center. I recognize it instantly.

"The Transit Light?" breathes Danielle.

"Bullshit," I say. "It's just a photo of the Transit Light." Even as the words leave my mouth, I know they're wrong. Xi doesn't play games.

"I don't have a photo of the Transit Light. This is the location app."

"What the hell," I mutter, retrieving my own phone. When I punch the app icon, I get the same result. Instead of a map, all I see is the circular light framed by the darkness. "How did you do this?" I ask, wondering if Xi somehow hacked Google's main network.

That quirky, sideways smile broadens. "I'm afraid you overestimate my technical abilities, Ohm. It's Quint. There's no other explanation."

On a hunch I turn up the volume on my phone. "Motherfucker," I chuckle when I hear the tone. "It's the Transit Frequency."

There it is—that vibratory rumble Quint would have us focus on during the tuning sessions. The tone was intended to facilitate our exit from the world of matter. It was our gateway to the realm of pure energy. I hadn't heard it in over a year. My heart begins to race.

Danielle takes my phone and holds it to her ear. "It sounds different to me. How can you be so sure?"

"That's the sonic signature. Quint and I were replicating it by running pictures of the Transit Light through a spectrometer. The idea was to convert the light waves into sound so we could broadcast it from the roof. I know this is it. It's got to be."

My guts start to rumble in unison with the sound, increasing my certainty.

"Why didn't I know about this?"

"I don't know, Danielle." I say, too distracted to worry about the jealousy creeping into her voice. "The more important question is, what the fuck is the Transit Light doing on the cellular network?"

Danielle retrieves her own phone and seems relieved to confirm the same result as the rest of us.

"I wonder…" she says. "Can you think of any other explanation, Xi?"

"Can I think of an explanation why a global satellite network would be compromised in this one location? I estimate we're about three kilometers from Quint's burial site. Presuming the interference is localized, I would suggest the coincidences are too numerous to be explained in any other way. Quint's remains are speaking to us from beyond the Transit Light."

Danielle stares at the screen for a moment, her eyes pooling with tears. She places her hand over her mouth to suppress a sob. "That's…That's just so beautiful. He's calling us home. Maybe it's not too late. Maybe he's opening a portal for us." She places a hand on my shoulder. "I'm sorry I've been after you, Simon. I just can't tell you how empty my life has been since he left. But this makes so much sense. He wouldn't just leave us behind like this. He had a reason for doing it this way. I just know it."

It amazes me how quickly she returns to the belief system that once dominated our lives for the better part of ten years. These two women are the closest to family I've ever had. Together we lived for one purpose. Everything since then has been meaningless darkness. After the others departed, I spent empty days watching normal people walk around and do normal shit. Their jobs, sporting events, and restaurants leave me feeling emptier by the day. Seeing the Transit Light feels like a reprieve from an execution.

"It's cool, Danielle," I say, studying the image on my phone. "No hard feelings…"

"Astra," she interrupts. "Call me Astra. Xi's right. I've always been Astra. I will be Astra to the end. I should never have doubted him."

"Are you sure?" I ask.

"I'm sure."

I hear the love in her voice.

And so, once again, Astra is reborn.

Putting my phone away, I realize we need another way to locate the address. It's not as if there are any street signs. It's hard to think with the racket of the insects competing with the sound of the motor. Staring out at the stark hillside, I am struck by the clarity of the sunlight. There are those times when everything is perfectly illuminated — this is one of those moments. I feel as if the messy clutter of the cosmos snaps into focus, making total sense. For the first time in over a year, I'm happy to be alive — happy that the bullet missed my brain.

That's when I notice the hawk. You see them from time to time, perched along the sides of the highways. They just sit there on tree limbs or telephone poles, watching traffic pass them by. This one's feathers are fluffed, accentuating its light brown plumage.

"Check out that hawk," I say, but the others are still absorbed by the Transit Light, listening to the hum on their phones. Just as I speak, the hawk spreads its wings and slowly drifts down from the trees above the SUV. "I bet it's going after a rabbit or something." Xi looks up just in time to see it execute a lazy turn toward our vehicle about fifty yards away.

"Look at that," I say, on the verge of tears myself. "It's got to be another sign. I wonder if that's a Blue Tail. Do you think Quint's awareness is strong enough to occupy the central nervous systems of the animals around here?"

No sooner have the words left my mouth than the hawk contracts itself into an aerodynamic missile and shoots directly toward us. I'm unable to speak. All I can see is the creature's face growing larger by the moment. It takes less than two seconds for it to cover the gap between us. I am struck by its intensely focused eyes, its look of predatory concentration. That's all I have time to consider before the hawk smashes into the windshield at over one hundred miles per hour. Astra screams and looks at the cracked, bloody glass. Feathers drift slowly earthward in the wake of the concussion.

Before I can say anything, Xi is out of the car. Astra and I watch as she gently scoops the hawk from the hood. I exit the vehicle hesitantly, looking skyward for another attack. I suddenly find myself sensing menace behind every tree. A crushed detergent bottle lays half-buried in the ditch alongside the road. When I come around to the front of the SUV, Xi is sitting cross-legged on the dirt road, cradling the hawk in her lap. I look just in time to see its head slump and its chest cease heaving.

"It departed in my hands," she says, looking at the two of us. "I was holding it, and then it departed its vehicle."

"You mean it died," I reply, but Astra puts a hand on my shoulder.

"Let's say a prayer," she says.

Xi hesitates for a moment, then places the dead hawk on the side of the road. It looks as if it's simply roosting. It's strange the way an old habit comes back to you so easily. I never thought I would ever participate in another ET ritual. Almost against my will, I find myself linking hands with the two women. We stand around the hawk in a circle.

"Just as I do not fear the sunrise," intones Astra.

"I will not fear death," Xi and I answer.

"Just as I do not fear the passing seasons."

"I will not fear the infirmity of my vehicle."

"For my body is a transient container."

"And my awareness will live forever as cosmic energy."

And so we're linked once again, at least for a moment. I can't count the hours that I meditated and prayed with these two women. We were once appendages of a single organism. For a moment, that unity is present once again. It's the type of connection that can't be experienced through mere cognition. It must be felt inside your body. Until you've experienced it, you will never understand.

"Thank you, Astra," says Xi. Her eyes are glassy, but I know she will not shed a tear. She has too much control for that. I'm beginning to wonder if we have set a trap for ourselves, but I say nothing as we return to the SUV. The real question I want to ask is, why would a hawk dive into the windshield of our car? But the need for that answer is irrelevant for my companions. They see the hawk as a transcendent moment. That's what Quint used to call them—one of those times when group unity supersedes all other considerations. Everything comes storming down on you with pure, diamond clarity. The hawk dove because it desired to leave its vehicle and, in that explosive moment, was freed from this earth. That's the way faith is. It's not up to the believers to prove their reality, but the skeptics to disprove it. As for me, I'm not really that inclined to lean one way or the other these days. If the story still works for them, then who am I to say otherwise?

~

I wouldn't know from personal experience, but I can imagine that spending the night in the San Bernardino Mountains with a bunch of Reichians can be kind of trippy. The only thing you know for sure is that you're going to experience some crazy shit. That's how Quint described his *mountaintop experience.* When he first came out to California, he hooked up with a residual cell of seekers who were influenced by Wilhelm Reich, a psychologist imprisoned and killed by the United States Government for promoting his theory of the orgone. Reich linked all cosmic energy to the orgasm, and orgones represented a universal vibratory pulse that, if harnessed correctly, would adjust the human body to universal orgasmic energy like a tuning fork. He figured that if everyone got plugged in, they wouldn't be so likely to gravitate toward fundamentalist religion and fascist dictators. So you can understand why the feds tried to burn his books after they killed him. It doesn't do to let the trained monkeys off the chain.

Quint didn't tell very many people that story. I remember the day he showed me and Astra the picture of himself sitting in one of those orgone accumulators. It was weird to see that younger version with a full head of hair. Back then he was just a kid searching for the truth like the rest of us.

But that night on the mountain changed him.

Six of them went out there with these giant cloudbusters. The devices looked like old-fashioned TV antennas. Those transmitters could harness orgone energy and direct it back toward the sky, producing all kinds of weird weather patterns. I don't think Quint ever fit in with the Reichians. He was too reserved. But he was also a seeker. That's the thing about a group like ET. We didn't internalize the crap being slung by the police state or the pulpits. It takes a lot of courage to look up at the skies and really see what's going on.

So Quint was up there on the mountain when they pointed their cloudbusters at this cumulus that was just getting ready to occlude Sirius. I guess they made contact with something. He heard the others talking, but couldn't decode anything they were saying. It was like he was being transcribed into the stars. He was everywhere and nowhere at the same time. Then everything went black. All that was left was that terrible hum.

When he regained consciousness, it was morning. The others were wandering around aimlessly. One woman had fallen into a crevice and wrecked her leg. He felt drained and his head hurt like a motherfucker. I remember when he showed me the scar on the side of his skull—it was just a straight white line. If you pressed on it, you could feel the indentation in the bone. Someone or something on that mountaintop had cut right into his brain.

The others weren't so lucky. Everything had been scrubbed from their hard drives. All they could do was stumble around, speaking nonsense words. Their entire language subsystem—the part of the brain that tells you how to use syntax—was destroyed. He staggered back to the car with these blinding flashes of light in his skull. Even years later he would still clutch his head in pain when a transmission came through from the mothership. Man, did he suffer for the rest of us. It always pissed me off when someone hassled him in public. That's fucked up, you know. These are the same people who think some magical being is running the show from an imaginary place called heaven. And they had the gall to fuck with Quint.

What is it about humans and their contempt for the truth?

Anyway, when he finally found help, the authorities rounded up his buddies. Their minds were gone—total ego death. They had no awareness left. That's the thing about the Transit Light; you need power to fuck with it. Otherwise, it will take everything you are. All five of them had to be institutionalized, unable to do anything but drool and bang their heads against the wall. By the time ET was making its final preparations for boarding, at least three of those poor people were dead. They just wasted away with nothing but feeding tubes to sustain them. It was a hard way to check out.

After that night on the mountaintop, Quint could *see*. He was awake. Those creatures had done something to him. They were like gods touching their prophet. And he was a good one. Quint would spend every waking moment serving their purpose, looking for others who had the ability to share in that terrible, wonderful journey.

Then there was the night he decided to show me what the final recycling would look like. He had this special way of sending image fragments by touching his forehead to yours. I thought I was ready for it after all the tuning sessions. But the sheer scope of the nightmare floored me. They were going to burn the whole planet. There was nothing benevolent about it. They were just wandering, indifferent gods. I thought about all those billions of people having matter and energy warped into an endless nightmare. Worst of all, they wouldn't simply die. The Transit Light was going to feed on their awareness, using it to fuel the ship. The Transit Light wasn't heaven…it was hell. It was a burning orb that devoured the screams of a billion lost souls the same way I might wolf down a cheeseburger.

In the end, I preferred a bullet to the truth.

After Quint departed, I thought it was all over—just a bad acid trip. But then came the call. It was more than guilt that led me to this wild place in the middle of the Ozark Mountains. It's true that Astra and Xi missed the boat because of my bullshit, so I figured I owed them. But now I'm not so sure. Maybe Quint was still testing me. So it's more than guilt; I need to know the truth. I want to know what's in the Transit Light.

~

I roll down the window and call to the guy sitting on the front step of a rusted trailer.

"Hey, bro! Can I talk to you for a minute?"

"Goddamn it, Simon," mutters Astra. We've pulled over to check the direction of the sun. That's when you know you're lost. It turns out that none of us are very good at orienteering. I never knew there could be so many dirt roads in one place; there were hundreds of miles of them snaking through the hills. The houses have become increasingly ramshackle, often consisting of nothing more than a camper shell. Some of the abandoned cars have been repurposed as trash containers or chicken coops.

"What's your problem, Astra?" I ask, annoyed, wiping the sweat from my forehead. The heat is making my wound itch. "We're fucking lost. Without a signal we might as well be on the moon."

"We've got a signal."

"Yeah, but it's not leading us anywhere."

"I just hate it when you get like this."

"Like what?"

"When you start talking to strangers. It's not cool. Haven't you noticed all the Confederate flags?"

I have noticed and they give me the creeps. But there's something about the way the guy watches us. He doesn't seem driven by dull hostility. He seems calm—almost intelligent.

Slowly he stands and begins walking toward the road, never taking his eyes off me. He's skinny and sports a dark goatee. He looks tired—like he's seen too much and carries a great burden. But there's also something hard about him, as if surviving in these hills has made him resourceful.

"God, he looks feral," complains Astra. "Xi, would you tell Simon to button this shit up."

There's a reason the space program specifies that three-person missions are problematic for interplanetary travel—you can't escape the two-against-one dynamic. But Xi is cut from unusual cloth. After a long pause she says, "I think it's best that I not serve as a mediating tool, Astra. You and

Ohm will work things out once you are in harmony with the Transit Frequency."

Astra glances at Xi in the rearview mirror, considering some form of protest. But she stops herself. I can see her listening deep inside and sensing the truth in Xi's words. These hills do emit a strange harmonic beneath the trash and debris. There's more here than brutal existence followed by an equally brutal death. But it's hard to pinpoint the harmonic because it's filtered through a topography of hunger and predation. We're all becoming increasingly tense, as if some powerful energy is growing inside our bodies, pushing up from geological depths.

The guy leans over me, placing one hand on the roof of the car.

"Hey, man," I say, smiling. "Sorry to bother you, but my friends and I are kind of lost."

He takes a long pause to assess each of us in turn, his green eyes carefully calculating the situation. I can tell he's not a guy who acts impulsively. Everything is measured with him.

"Looks like you had a little accident," he says, touching the bloody, cracked windshield.

"Dude, a fucking hawk dove straight into our car."

He nods. If he considers the explanation difficult to credit, he gives no indication.

"I figure you're looking for the Boatwright Cemetery," he says, his voice marked by the hill dialect. We sit stunned for a moment.

"That's right, man. How did you guess that?"

"I've seen that before," he says, glancing toward Xi.

"What?" I ask, still confused.

"He means my emblem," says Xi. She points to the starburst insignia over her left breast. It's our symbol. Everything in ET revolved around the Transit Light. "So you've seen this before?" she asks.

"On that new headstone at the Boatwright Cemetery," he replies, glancing up at the relentless sun for a moment, as if gauging its movement. The locusts crackle in the weeds around us and a blue jay complains in the distance. "It doesn't take a genius to put two and two together."

"So you know where it is?" I ask.

He nods.

"That's great! Can you direct us?"

His eyes come back to me.

"You're the one who shot himself." As he speaks, I notice his voice is distant, like a shock victim. I wonder what's happened to this guy, then I look around at the slow-motion catastrophe that he calls home. It would be enough to fuck with anyone.

"So you know who we are?" asks Astra.

"I read about it on the news website. There was a little bit of a stir when folks heard they were bringing Cody back here to bury him. Not everyone was thrilled about it. But they put him in there all the same. They got a big old headstone over him, like he was some kind of war hero or something. It's got one of those stars on it, just like the one on your friend's shirt."

Cody.

It's weird to hear Quint's pre-awakened name.

"Yeah. We'd like to pay our respects. We're not staying or anything. We don't want to upset anyone," I say, trying to assuage his suspicion. To my surprise, he laughs.

"You can't really upset people any more than they already are, but I appreciate the sentiments."

"What do you mean?"

"You can't feel it?"

Of course we can feel it. The place is vibrating with fear and anticipation. It's like listening to tinfoil rubbed against sandpaper. The more I try to relax, the more I find myself tensing up. It's like I'm waiting for something to happen—for some kind of attack. He watches the comprehension on my face, and his smile broadens.

"Yeah, you can feel it," he says by way of confirmation.

Xi leans forward slightly. "My name is Xi. This is Astra and Ohm, though he prefers to be called Simon. Do you think you could help us?"

He turns to her like an owl watching a mouse dart across a field. "Maybe. My name is Caleb. Caleb Starnes. But I don't think my directions would be any good. You're at least three miles from where you need to be. There's at least six turns. The cemetery is about a quarter-mile from the road through a cow pasture."

"You're shitting me," says Astra.

"I shit you not."

We sit in silence for a moment. The thought of driving around these endless dirt roads isn't appealing. Risking Astra's wrath, I say, "You think you could show us?"

To my surprise, she doesn't object. She must be as sick of this place as I am.

Caleb glances back at the trailer. "Hmmm... Seeing as how I'm kind of busy at the moment, it's gonna cost you fifty bucks. Everything out here might look like shit, but it ain't free."

~

I approach the old farmhouse with our new friend. It sits amid a cluster of sycamores alongside a dried creek bed. The structure is classic 1930s and I can't help but notice the railings are solid oak. Other than the vinyl siding someone draped over it at some point in the past, its stately façade stands out amid the blistered landscape. It must have been a nice place at some point, but time has taken its toll. I notice the window frames are starting to rot.

Caleb walks ahead of me while Astra and Xi wait in the SUV. According to our guide, the cemetery sits on the other side of a cow pasture behind the house. There's a gate we can drive through, but you have to be blood kin to access the site without permission. During the ride over, Caleb seemed to take an interest in Xi, as if she was some weird action figure dropped from the sky. I figure that's a good sign. The guy is curious, and curiosity is always better than blind faith.

"So, did you know Quint?" I still can't bring myself to say his pre-awakened name.

Cody.

"No, but I have a couple of cousins who went to school with him. They said he was religious, but not in a good way, if you know what I mean."

It bothers me that he has access to a part of Quint we never knew. I look around at the withered trees and dried-up streambed, trying to picture this place as the breeding ground for the one true prophet.

"Did he ever show signs? You know…Of being special?"

Caleb pauses at the bottom step to the house, eyeing me for a moment. He adjusts a camo hat that covers his dark hair. "You know how it is with messiahs. It's hard to work miracles in your hometown."

"What?" The guy is always making private jokes, talking in a code only he understands.

"Don't you read the Bible?"

"A little," I confess. Quint always focused on the passages about fires in the sky or resurrection.

"The Book of Mark. When Jesus returned to his hometown after he was famous everyone was real anxious to meet him. They had all heard about this really great preacher that worked all kinds of miracles, but when they got a look at him, they laughed. It was only the carpenter's son. Then that poor old boy wasn't able to work a single miracle." Caleb cracks a yellowed smile.

"I hadn't heard that one," I reply. I have to confess that I didn't expect to find anyone back here but a bunch of uneducated Holy Rollers. But, then again, I guess I'm one to talk. The guy who misses his ride on the flying saucer really doesn't have a lot of room for prejudice.

My thoughts dissipate when the smell hits me. You can almost taste it from the steps. It's the smell of rotting flesh. Caleb hesitates at the front door, its paint chipping and knob hanging askew. Then he knocks.

"Mr. Miller? Mrs. Miller? It's Caleb Starnes!" he calls. "Got some folks here that want to visit the cemetery." He waits a few seconds, then steps back.

"Maybe they're not home," I suggest, bringing a rag to my nose.

He glances at the ancient Chevy pick-up in the driveway, then shakes his head. Without a word he scans the tree line slowly, as if looking for an ambush. Then he pops a pill in his mouth.

"What's that?"

"Xanax. You don't think I could stand being this close to *it* sober," he says, biting off his words. I think about all the Oxy I've been downing. I haven't actually had that much pain. It's something else. There's a sickness in the air. It makes you want to crawl out of your skin and leave your carcass for the worms.

"What's that smell, Caleb? It can't be spoiled food. Could it?"

He doesn't say anything for a moment, just stands there stroking his beard. Then he nods his head, as if settling some inner debate. "We best be getting on down the road."

"But we came here to see Quint. There's no way I'm leaving when we're this close. It's just a quarter mile through the pasture."

"Mister," he says. "This is a bad situation."

"Well fuck," I say, motioning to my companions in the car.

The guy is in for a surprise if he thinks I'm going to leave because of a bad smell. You see, I see things differently since I shot myself. According to my neurologist, the concussion from the gunshot damaged my frontal lobe. I never really had great impulse control to start with, but since my suicide attempt, it's all I can do to restrain myself from doing things that most people find embarrassing or disturbing. If I feel like doing something, I do it. I really don't give a shit if someone else thinks it's transgressive.

I push the door open, calling into the shadows. "Hello! My name is Simon. Is everyone OK?" It takes a moment for my good eye to adjust to the dim light.

The world looks different when you have monocular vision. As I glance around the room, it appears that the dust motes are passing through the objects around them—the shredded couch, the reclining chair, the ancient TV. I've developed a new appreciation for light now that my eyes are no longer able to calculate distance based on the triangulation of data from two optical points. As a result, light seems to flow through a single field. It's as if I no longer perceive a difference between photons and matter.

"That's a damn good way to catch a chest full of buckshot," warns Caleb over my shoulder. "You ain't in California."

I point to the mask.

"I've already had my dance with death, so I'm not too worried about it, brother. The fucker upstairs knows where to find me when he wants to call me home." Then I laugh.

Soon I'm able to discern a pattern to the clutter. There are the usual things one expects to see in a house. Clothes and toys are strewn on the floor. But there's something else. In one corner I perceive an assortment of tools, and there are two saw horses standing side by side in the main room with an assortment of lumber on the floor. I bend down and examine the wood, turning it in my hands. It's from the barn outside.

"I know a buddy of mine back home who would cry if he saw how they tore up this wood. Look at that weathering. He reclaims old barn wood for rich fucks who want to give their houses that faux country look. He would've paid good money for this."

"You just walked in here without an invitation?"

It's Astra, standing with her hands on her hips. Xi lurks behind her like some acolyte, the dust motes giving the claustrophobic impression of cheap incense. Sweat is pouring down my face, stinging my eye.

"What in God's name is that awful stench?" Astra asks, putting a hand to her nose.

The room is sweltering. Someone has placed tinfoil in the windows to deflect the unrelenting sunlight. When I open my mouth to answer, I see the nails protruding from a closet door.

"What the fuck is this?" I say, examining the frame.

The points of the nails are sticking straight out, as if they've been driven by someone inside. I run my finger gently across one of the sharpened points.

"This is really fucked up," I whisper to myself. I

feel Astra's hand on my shoulder.

"Simon, stop."

"What's the matter?" I reply. "You chickening out? In for a penny, in for a pound." My words come out a little more bitter and sarcastic than I intend. I know she's scared. I can feel my own heart racing as I push against the closet door. The wood is thin, but reinforced from the inside.

"Try this." I turn around to find Xi handing me a crowbar. She usually has a look of calm bemusement on her face. Now her lips are twisted into that tight smirk she gets when something worries her. It takes several blows before I can get the edge of the crowbar under the door. No one in the room says a word. It seems like the only sound in the universe is the splintering of ancient timber. Soon I am faltering in the heat, never having fully recovered my stamina after such a long hospitalization. I feel my strength starting to flag and vision going black.

"Christ, give it to me!"

Panting, I'm only too happy to relinquish the crowbar to Astra, who tears into the door with more precision. Within about five minutes, she has pried it away from the wall along with about half the frame. After she looks inside, her eyes glaze and she turns back to me, upset.

"There...I hope you're fucking happy," she says to me, as if the tragic tableau is my fault. The three of us wave our hands in the air, fending off the storm of flies that erupts from the freshly opened crypt. Inside are the bloated, decayed bodies of four people—two adults and two children. The advanced stage of decomposition makes immediate gender identification impossible. Their skin is blackened and bodies distended by gas. There is a certain democracy in death; it spares no one. The bodies are huddled in the back corner, as if trying to protect themselves from an intruder. The full realization of the situation dawns on me.

"They just boarded themselves up in here?" says Astra, her voice dripping with outrage. Her skin glows with the sheen of perspiration. I watch a maggot drop from a child's mouth. The stench of putrescence hovers in the air and I wonder if there is any amount of scrubbing that could ever wash that odor away.

Xi steps past both of us, seemingly unbothered by the smell. She produces a latex glove and snaps it on. Before I have time to wonder why she would be carrying such a thing, she has lifted the face of one child from its mother's shoulder. The skin is flattened on the side where its cheek was resting. As

I stare into those sightless sockets, I am acutely aware of what awaits us all at the end of the night. This is why we pursue the Transit Light. There's got to be something more to it. It takes an effort to stop from grinding my teeth.

"I don't see any signs of trauma," says Xi, her voice edged with a hint of tension. "Given the temperature in this room, I am guessing death would have come as a result of dehydration or heat stroke."

"That's impossible," retorts Astra. "No one would board themselves up in a closet with two small children and just die. Who does that?"

Xi turns to face Astra. The two women lock eyes for a long moment before Xi speaks.

"I know you're upset, Astra. But I'm afraid we must assume that the situation is much worse than we thought."

That's what I love about Xi. She's not a fan of bullshit.

Things *are* a lot worse.

~

We're standing around the SUV. All of us but Xi are smoking cigarettes borrowed from our guide. It's not only for our nerves, but to mask the smell. While we were in the house Caleb explored the pasture, finding a portion of barbed wire fence collapsed under the weight of the livestock. It appears the entire herd tried to push its way through, pulling the posts from the ground. Their bodies were lacerated in the effort. Once hopelessly entangled, they died. Now the cows lay rotting under the afternoon sun just like the bodies in the house. I have to turn away when Caleb thrusts a stick up one of the cow's noses, causing the gas inside of the body to escape with a sputtering sound along with a vomit of blood.

"Are we going to call the cops?" asks Astra, now surprisingly calm. She stares into the distance.

"I don't know if they would come," says Caleb. "They done lost two men in this area over the last three months and they aren't real friendly these days." He traces the ground with his bloody stick. "Besides, there's no one to call." He holds up his phone. It too displays the undulating image of the Transit Light.

"We can still drive to town."

"I'm not sure you get what I'm saying. They're not real partial to me and I can tell you for a fact they're not gonna like any of you. You're liable to end up in the White River. Your best bet is to take me home and forget you ever set foot out here."

"I'm afraid that's not an option," replies Xi,

cocking her head to one side. "Our mission is deeply spiritual."

The guide laughs and shakes his head.

"Spiritual? And just what is your mission anyway?"

For a moment you can hear nothing but the buzzing of the locusts. Somewhere in the distance a jackass brays spasmodically. One of the dead cows makes a sloppy farting noise. Under normal circumstances I might have laughed, but the whole situation is just too macabre. The racket makes me feel small. It's interesting how we can spend our lives blowing our own problems out of proportion when nature is out there, waiting. It doesn't care how you're feeling today. It's full of creatures that want to drink your blood or feast on your dead flesh. The whole shitshow is neither good nor bad, just relentlessly predatory.

"I saw tools in the back of your Subaru," Caleb prompts. I hadn't thought about that. I guess it does look kind of suspicious to visit a cemetery with a car full of shovels and picks.

"We're here to take him home." It's Xi who speaks first.

Caleb nods. "That's what I figured. You're thinking to dig that old boy up—take him back to

UFO country?"

"It's a little more than that," she replies, the beginnings of that sideways smile breaching the surface. "You might say we were called to this task."

Caleb studies her for a moment. There doesn't seem to be any judgment in his face. The three of us are accustomed to rejection by outsiders—the usual reactions range from bemusement to open hostility. ET's ideas agitate something deep inside most people, whose own religious biases are coded way down in their DNA. Anything to the contrary is met with contempt. But Caleb doesn't flinch.

"We used to have these tuning sessions," I begin, studying the old barn with the panels ripped from one side. "It was kind of like meditation, but different. We didn't focus on our breathing or try to detach our feelings from the inevitable thought flow. The Transit Light emits a specific sonic signature. That's how we were signaling it."

"You mean the UFO ship?" I study his words for any sign of judgment. Nothing.

"Sort of. It's not a ship in the way you've been trained to think about it. It's not like *Star Wars* or something like that. This ship is pure light. Its crew intermingles with the light. We were going to be converted to pure, plasma energy. Can you imagine that? No more human body. No more pain. No more sadness. No more waking up with crippling headaches. The Transit Light transcends the realm of matter. We were trying to plug into that eternal vibratory frequency."

Caleb stares, unblinkingly.

"So, you still believe all that?" he asks. "I mean, you shot yourself before your friends took off. Ain't that right? That's what the news said, unless they got it wrong."

I look back at the barn, struggling with the lump rising in my chest.

"Simon had a crisis of faith," says Astra, her voice flat. Finding the dead family has temporarily depleted her antagonistic energy.

"So, Simon, you're not so sure anymore." Then he turns to Xi. "I know you're a believer."

"Quint was like a tuning fork," she replies. "He would emit sonic vibrations during the tuning sessions. We would align our central nervous systems to that frequency. The Transit Signal can be distressing for the uninitiated. So the sessions could be very…energetic."

"You mean he made noise?"

"That's right. The human body is equipped with blocking mechanisms. Child-rearing in our society is nothing but a regime for downloading prejudicial software. They want children to live in terror of the unknown, so they will never reach their true potential. That's why it takes so much practice. The consciousness must be carefully prepared for departure from a vehicle that knows nothing but fear and anxiety. If your central nervous system isn't correctly aligned, you will be completely obliterated when the Transit Light converts your mind into pure energy. The idea is to allow your awareness to make the leap intact."

Caleb discards his bloody stick and takes one last pull on the cigarette.

"You got the part about child-rearing right. What did you mean when you said these sessions were energetic?"

"Shit would happen," says Astra, her voice still distant. "Glass would break. People would get nosebleeds. Sometimes they would go into convulsions and we would have to restrain them." Then she looks at Caleb, her eyes suddenly present. "But it was hardest on Quint. His human vehicle wasn't designed for that level of stress. It hurt him deep inside. You see, they gave him the gift of being able to transmit the frequency, but with that gift came great pain."

Caleb shakes his head. "Poor Cody. Who would have thought he would end up like that?"

"He hasn't ended," says Astra, the force of conviction returning to her voice. "We all started picking up the vibration about a week ago. It wasn't much; kind of like a gnat buzzing in your ear. That's when we knew he was calling us. The closer we got to this spot, the louder and more intense the frequency."

Then she holds up her cellphone, allowing the hum to mingle with the roar of the insects.

"Quint," is all she says by way of explanation.

"So you figure his body is sending out that signal? That's what's got everyone and everything on edge in these hills? Just the other day an old gal named Dana dropped her newborn in the burn barrel—said the world was too cruel for him."

"Cortisol," says Xi. "It's the fear hormone inside the human body. It's a good bet that every living thing in this area is inundated by it. It's the natural response of a vehicle that hasn't been trained to process the Transit Signal."

"So that's why you're so calm."

"Oh, I feel it." Xi smirks again, a bit of Scottish accent coming into her voice. "I've just trained my vehicle not to resist. The key is not to fight it. It's not easy, but I don't require a chemical aid like Xanax."

Caleb stands and hitches his dusty jeans, studying the horizon. Then he turns to me and I can feel his eyes tracing the contours of my mask, as if he's trying to penetrate it with his eyes. It usually makes me nervous when people stare at me like that, but the guy has a right to know what he's getting himself into.

He turns back to Xi. "I don't mind telling you that's some messed-up shit you just said. But I guess it's no more messed-up than most of what I heard growing up around here. I'll tell you what—I'll keep your little secret. Hell, I'll even help you dig old Cody up. I got just one condition. You take me with you."

"Whoa," says Astra, instantly suspicious. "Why would you want to do that?"

"Look around you. Everyone I know who's worth a shit has already pulled up stakes and moved. My old lady ran off to her relatives in Wesley. Can't say I was sorry to see her go. When you drove by, I was just sitting here, trying to figure out what the hell I was doing here. Then here came the three of you." He pauses for moment, dropping his eyes.

"Maybe shit happens for a reason."

"Everything happens for a reason," says Xi. "We

just need to read the signs."

"You know we're headed back to Malibu," says Astra, still suspicious. "We don't have time for homesickness."

"I hear you. There ain't nothing here for me. There never has been."

One of the strange things about living with a group like ET is that you find converts in the most unexpected places. I step forward and extend my hand.

"Welcome aboard, brother," as my laughter booms across the hillside. "You know you just fucked up. Right?"

~

"Is it Quint?" Astra's eyes are glassy with rage, her hand covering her mouth.

"I don't think so," I reply. "This guy still has some hair."

The corpse has been skewered through the pelvis on one of those tall, pointed grave markers. Its jaw is hanging wide open and flies orbit the gruesome display in an angry snarl. One desiccated arm lies discarded to one side, still encased in a tattered coat sleeve. The ants are greedily claiming this prize. I step a little closer.

"I think it's a guy."

"Deputy Gentry," says Caleb, hanging behind me, his skin waxen.

"The guy who got killed back in here?"

"An old farmer named T.A. Littrel got to shooting people's livestock. Chickens, pigs, horses. He kept saying something about heaven being just for people, not animals. When the deputy showed up to stop him, he got a .30-06 to the face for his trouble."

I look closer and see where the jaw has been wired to the skull by the undertaker. People and their open-casket funerals.

"Not the best cosmetic work I've ever seen," I say, laughing.

"Doesn't that make you sick to be so close to it, Simon?" says Astra.

"No. Not really. Just kind of sad. He was alive, then he wasn't."

I don't know why dead bodies fail to bother me. They're messy more than anything else. When Quint explained that they were just organic vehicles for our consciousness, it made perfect sense. A decaying corpse was nothing more than an abandoned car rusting in the sun. The bigger question is why someone would take the time to dig this man up and stick him on top of a monument. There's something vaguely sexual about the pose that bothers me.

"Could be a warning," I say, prodding it with the toe of my shoe.

"Hard to say," says Caleb, looking around at the hills. "People back here have been getting more black-hearted and crazy by the day. Can't say this is doing much for my nerves either."

"Just remember that cortisol only has a half-life of one hour," says Xi in a comforting tone. "The fear and anxiety will pass."

"Holy shit," I say as a maggot the size of a golf ball drops from underneath the dress shirt. The fat, pale creature wriggles vigorously in the grass, as if enraged at being denied its meal. "Look at the size of that maggot. It's huge. And look at it move."

Before I have a chance to study it further, Caleb's sneaker crushes it underfoot, popping it like an overripe fruit. "That ain't no fly larvae. I don't know what the hell that is, but no fly produces a brood like that. There ain't no sense in looking at it."

As dark thought occurs to me. Perhaps the entire cemetery has been desecrated. I look up and notice gravestones lying toppled or smashed from one end to the other. The country cemetery can't be more than fifty plots. Almost everyone in it is some sort of kin to one another. Most of the stones are ancient and lichen-encrusted. A few are the newer, gray marble types. A couple are marked for double occupancy, though the date of death remains blank on one side. Sometimes the living tarry in the sunlight too long, leaving the departed to rot in the ground for decades. At least half of the markers are damaged.

"Who would do this?" I wonder aloud, though the question seems stupid the moment I voice it. This is what the Transit Signal does when it's beamed into the vehicles of the uninitiated. Their primitive consciousness provides them with just enough awareness to perceive that something is wrong, but rather than use it to evolve to the next level, they regress to barbarism. At least someone around here was sensitive enough to identify this place as the epicenter of the problem, but their reaction was not to understand the source of their pain. Instead they lashed out at everything in sight. They wanted to turn the cemetery into a reflection of their own personal nightmare.

As we enter the small cemetery, I am struck by how lonely it is. There's a section dedicated to infants that died at or near birth. Right next to this is another patch of ground marking the young mothers who departed while pushing them into the world. The perimeter is rimmed by trees on three sides and, in many places, the brush has reclaimed certain graves. It isn't well-manicured like the cemeteries back home, but someone has been trimming the weeds around the markers occasionally. Still, the briars and thistles encroach on all sides.

To the west, it's a different story. The ground slopes and the trees have been cleared, treating us to a panoramic view of the valley. The mountains are double-edged like that. Usually, I feel nothing but claustrophobic anxiety at the vegetation pushing toward me on all sides, as if to suffocate any living thing that strays into its domain. Then there are occasional moments of beauty like this one. But the reprieve is only temporary as the drone of the insects deafens me, creating a kind of cranial pressure.

"Any of you have any idea why Cody wanted to come back here to be buried? It wasn't like he had much use for his kin once he came of age."

Caleb's question dangles out there in front of all three of us.

"I think he was looking for a place where no one would find him," says Astra, walking with arms folded among the desecrated gravestones. She stoops and returns one broken marker to its rightful place. "You have no idea how bad the press was back in Malibu. They would have hounded him after death. His gravesite would have become a national curiosity for religious nuts and potheads."

There she goes, making excuses for him. I can't help thinking about the way he deserted his flock. He should have ended up in the mass grave with the rest of them.

Then she turns to Caleb. "By the way, his name is Quint. It's short for Quintessence. He was the fabric that linked the cosmos—the bridge between matter and energy."

Caleb nods. "So if I stick around long enough, I'll get a new name as well."

She smiles. "That's the way it goes with us. By the way, where is Quint? I'm going to be heartbroken if some redneck has already dragged him from the earth. It's best just to get it over with. Where is he?"

Caleb motions to the east. "They put him back there in the brush. I guess they didn't really want him in here with the normal folks. But his estate paid in cash so they found a little something for him at the very edge of the property."

I'm holding my breath as we pick our way through the weeds toward the back of the cemetery. I know that if Quint ended up like the deputy, our plans will be destroyed. The thought sickens me. Just for once, I would like some clear answers. At length we come to a great marker, masked by a phalanx of poke and honeysuckle. Thank God for that. We study the soil for signs of disturbance. It has the look of being turned, but no more so than one might expect from a newer grave. I allow my muscles to relax. Ironically, the cemetery owner's efforts to marginalize Quint may have saved him.

Xi runs her hand across the marker, which reads: *Quintessence Boatwright, We Saw His Star.*

His marker is the largest in the cemetery. The massive piece of granite seems just as puzzling to me as Quint having himself shipped way out here. He was never a person given to material excess, so the expenditure strikes me as grotesque. Quint was as close to a mendicant preacher as one can find these days. Xi kneels and traces the Transit Star insignia carved into the center of the stone. It reminds me of the masonic symbols we passed while traversing the plots.

"*We saw his star.* I wonder what that means," she whispers.

"Matthew," says Caleb. "The star of Bethlehem." Then he gives a quick little smile. "Come to think of it, there are three of you. But, I guess you come from the west and not the east. Still, that's a peculiar coincidence."

Xi cocks her head and frowns. She was never entirely comfortable with Quint's biblical inclinations. Her own spiritual journey began with a far more secular and pragmatic religion. You don't have much use for God when you are placing your faith in dilithium crystals. While I study the jarring contrast between the marker and the man upon whom it sits, Astra returns to the SUV, traversing the narrow access trail that encompasses the cemetery. She moves the car to a secluded spot under a gnarled hickory near the grave. By now the sun is dropping in the sky, sitting like an angry furnace on the horizon.

As we prepare to dig, Xi begins to disrobe. This startles me, as I have never seen her do this, but I understand the necessity; the heat and humidity are almost beyond endurance. Underneath her uniform she wears a white tee-shirt and gym shorts. She neatly folds her uniform and places it in the back of the vehicle. Her skin is pale, like mine. After five surgeries and nearly six months in the hospital, this trip across the country is the first time I've had any real exposure to the sun in almost a year. Already my skin is beginning to redden.

That's when I notice the beekeeper. He exits the tree line on one side of the cemetery and trudges around its circumference about forty yards from where we stand. If he sees us, he gives no indication. Then I realize he's not a beekeeper. The blocky headgear is not a veil, but a welding mask. And the nozzle he carries in his hand is probably not a smoker.

"Who the fuck is that?" says Astra, instantly alert. "The last thing I need right now is to get busted for grave-robbing way out here in crackertown."

Caleb gives her a sideways glance. "Look around you. Does it look like the law has been making regular visits to this place? They don't want no part of this."

"It's not the law I'm worried about," she hisses. "White people have no trouble finding justice in anything they do. You should know that."

"Would you guys shut up," I interrupt. "I think that guy is wearing a compressed air tank on his back."

The figure comes to the grisly display at the entrance to the cemetery. He appears to look the grim statuary up and down, though it's hard to tell because his face is obscured. Then he steps back and points the nozzle at the corpse. Almost at once flame leaps out in front of him, drenching the exposed remains.

"Holy shit," says Astra, her voice now strangely calm.

"Yep," I say. "Can't say I expected that."

He continues to circle the display, hosing it from every angle, occasionally turning the fire toward the ground. Soon a dark, inky smoke is trailing into the sky. Even at a distance I can smell the kerosene.

Xi comes alongside me. "A homemade flamethrower. Perhaps he thinks the disturbances are the result of some type of infection."

As she speaks, bits of the corpse begin dropping to the ground in flaming chunks. I have to give the guy credit—the contraption may be crude, but it's sure effective. Soon another scent is carried on the wind.

"You know what that smell is," I laugh. "That's roasted deputy."

"Shut the fuck up, Simon," says Astra. "You're gonna really think it's funny if that asshole decides you're infected. A bullet to the brain isn't anything compared to burning to death."

The sharp comment sobers me. I open my mouth, then shut it. Maybe I had it coming. I reach into my pocket for another Oxy, the titanium plate in my head vibrating painfully.

Once the corpse is reduced to smoldering embers, the man begins moving in our direction, the flamethrower still clutched in one hand. He gives the impression of a farmer simply going about his daily chores, spraying tomato vines against the onset of spring beetles. When he's about ten feet away he pauses, studying us inscrutably through the welding helmet.

"Samson," says Caleb by way of greeting. I am relieved that our guide seems to know this flame-jockey.

Slowly a gloved thumb moves under the mask and slides it back, revealing the face an older man. His skin is sweaty and soiled from the exertion and heat. He has bright blue eyes that seem to look right past us.

"Caleb?" he replies. "Cynthia's boy."

Caleb nods.

"Well it's been a month of Sundays."

"Yes, sir," Caleb replies. I can sense the caution in his voice. "This is Mr. Samson Brody," he continues for our benefit. "He lives up yonder. Looks after the cemetery."

"That's right," says the man, his eyes finally focusing on us for the first time. They look distant and wild, like someone suffering from extreme dementia.

Caleb shifts nervously, his eyes glued to the flamethrower. "I just wanted you to know we didn't have nothin' to do with that—or knocking down those stones. These are just some folks come to pay respects to their kin."

Caleb's words strike me as ridiculous. We've already unloaded the Subaru. The ground is cluttered with shovels, picks, and crowbars. The man's eyes dance across the tools, then toward the blazing sun.

"You got to put fire to them." His voice is calm, as if explaining some mundane chore related to animal husbandry. "There ain't no other way. Whatever you dig up, you got to burn. The ground's alive, you see. It's vomiting up the dead. They're coming right up to choke the life out of us like we was newborn calves with the umbilical cord around our necks."

His eyes search ours one at a time. No one says anything.

"I ain't joking. Don't go poking down there unless you're going to put fire to it."

Caleb clears his throat. "Yes, Mr. Brody, we'll sure follow your advice."

The man studies our guide for a moment, then

nods his head sagely.

"Well, see that you do." Then he turns his back and we watch as he marches toward the tree line, a pyrokinetic knight patrolling his private necropolis. Once he disappears, we simply stand there, marveling at the vicissitudes that brought us to this place. The unreality of our situation comes crashing home for me, and I feel a little faint.

"So," I say at length. "And I thought we had some weirdos in L.A."

"A-fucking-men to that," replies Astra.

We laugh to release the tension. Even Xi joins in. Then, one by one, we grasp the hilts of the digging tools. All around us the cicadas are giving way to the katydids, signaling the approaching night.

~

The digging is tougher than expected. I take the first shift, but it doesn't take long before I'm gassed. The roots seem to grasp the end of the pick, as if they are animate things trying to suck me down into the earth. Like I said, this is a hungry place. The raw earth gives off an unfamiliar, acrid smell. Soon I am sitting cross-legged on the ground, panting like a foxhound; I had no idea how much my body deteriorated over the past year. It takes months, sometimes years to recover from an injury like mine.

Before long, Astra and Caleb replace me. The rush of air burns my windpipe until I'm able to calm my breathing. I try to make up for my infirmity by offering water to the diggers.

"What kind of soil is this, Caleb?" asks Astra, wiping away sweat with her shirt. She bends down and examines one of the roots. "This one's almost an inch thick."

"I don't know. There shouldn't be anything in here but feelers. I don't get the chance to dig lots of graves, but I'm pretty sure it's not supposed to be this hard."

I smack mosquitoes landing on my exposed flesh under the lamplight, each one leaving a tiny, bloody smear in its wake. The woods are alive with creatures that want to drink my blood or borough inside my body. I suddenly miss the wind blowing off the ocean back home. Up until now, mosquitoes had been more of a theoretical threat rather than a material one. I had never realized the number of ways in which that breeze protected us, driving the silent-winged assassins toward the interior.

"Damn," says Caleb, pulling out his pill container. "That was my last one."

"They won't do you much good this close to the source," advises Astra. "The best thing to do is to accept the signal. The more you fight, the more anxiety it produces. Those Xanax only work for a couple of hours, then drop you like stone. The backside is always worse."

Caleb takes a few more swings with the pick, then Astra moves in to remove the dirt he's loosened with the shovel. "You sound like you're speaking from experience."

Astra doesn't look up when she answers. "I was married once. He was a copyright attorney and I sold real estate. We had a son. Then a drunk driver swept out of the darkness and claimed them. You know that guy walked away without a scratch. Why does it always seem to happen that way? Anyway, I couldn't seem to do anything but cry after that. How do normal people do it? How do they live with the brutality of the world? I know what it's like — constantly looking for ways to disconnect your brain. But you can't escape yourself. After that night, my mind was a personal hell that just followed me around, engulfing me until all I could do was dream about total oblivion."

I know little about Astra's past. I certainly didn't know this. Something about the physical labor seems to loosen her tongue. Xi and I sit on the edge of the hole, listening and watching.

"So I took whatever I could get my hands on. No uppers, mind you. Pretty soon five or six milligrams of Xanax did nothing but keep me from climbing the walls. That's when I found black-tar heroin. The two together did the trick for a while. I was trying to kill the feelings inside my vehicle. But that's what your vehicle is designed to do. *Feel.* Then I met Quint and that all changed. The Transit Light became my total focus. It held out the promise that the pain wouldn't go on forever. One day, I would find a vehicle that was incapable of knowing grief."

Caleb swings the pick a few more times, then curses as it snags on another tree root. "I know what you mean about wanting to leave your body. When my daddy would whip me, I had this trick I could do where I just kind of went limp. I would let my mind wander. But that old man knew how to wield the limb. He could sense me trying to escape. Then he would really get going. He could always drag me back to earth with the pain. I guess I've spent my whole life trying to get out of my body — or vehicle."

"That's why ET is here. We all have similar stories. Seekers aren't born. The world makes them. People hurt you until there is no other choice. We're not eccentrics. We're driven from our bodies by the world."

"What is it about exhuming a corpse that breeds such intimacy?" I ask, and everyone laughs. Then I turn to Xi. "I don't remember you ever talking about your past. What led you to the Transit Light?"

She peers over the rim of the hole, studying the progress like one who has gambled their 401K on one throw of the dice. "It was nothing quite so dramatic for me. I just looked around at our species and figured we could do better. We're a rather sad lot, you know. There must be a level above human. It would be such a tragic waste if we were nothing but conversant primates doomed to breed ourselves out of existence through greed and stupidity. Quint was an example of what our species could achieve. His was the pathway to the level above."

As the night deepens, Astra climbs from the hole to give Xi a turn with the shovel. "Except we're not a whole lot closer to him. We can't have made more than two feet," says Astra, taking the water I offer. "This Arkansas clay is something. It's like the ground doesn't want to give him up."

Caleb and Xi take up the rhythm, one swinging the pick and the other taking out the loose soil. "I'm not as good at this as Astra," she admits. "Back at the headquarters she did most of the gardening. I'm afraid my chief responsibility was website design."

74

"You're doing fine," says Caleb. "I just wish I could get rid of the anxiety."

"Remember, it's only a chemical reaction in your vehicle. Just focus on the signal. You can feel it as a kind of vibration in your muscles—"

Xi's exposition is cut short when Caleb jumps out of the hole.

"Goddamn!" he yells.

"What's wrong?" I ask, moving in his direction.

"Something bit me."

"You hurt?"

"No! I mean, it bit my shoe."

I shine the light on the heel of his sneaker and detect a series of slashes in the rubber.

"Damn," I say. "What do you think, Astra? Maybe a mole."

"Moles aren't strong enough to shred rubber."

"It's nasty, whatever it is," says Caleb, walking around in a circle to work off some nervous energy. The signal is really starting to jangle his nerves. I can't say it's doing much for mine either. I look around at the shadows, sensing a threat behind every tree. Still, there's the constant hum of the insects. All the mammals and birds have cleared out. Nothing but the brainless invertebrates remain, rising in agitated swarms to attack whatever warm-blooded creatures have been stupid enough to stay.

Then something in the hole catches my eye. "Turn out the light, Astra."

"Why? Isn't it dark enough for you already?"

"Just humor me."

She switches off the work lamp and we're shrouded in darkness. There's no moon, and the stars are occluded by an oppressive haze. I study the hole, allowing my eyes to adjust.

"Well…" prompts Astra.

"Well, look," I say, motioning to the hole. Xi bends over the glowing patch of ground, examining it with her spade.

"That's strange," she says. "Could it be some type of radium?"

"No, man," I reply, getting down on my knees for a closer look. "This stuff is pure white. Radium is green."

Before I can say anything, Xi dips her finger in the gel. "It seems to be oozing out of this aperture," she says. Then the Scottish accent returns. "You might want to take a look at this. It looks like the Big Guy is sending us a message." She holds it aloft, allowing it to drip from her fingers like syrup. I rub my good eye to clear my vision.

"Am I the only one seeing this?" I ask.

"Damn," says Astra, peering over my shoulder. "It's beautiful."

At first, I think the particles suspended inside the liquid are tiny air bubbles, but when I look closer, I notice they're moving. They seem to spin around one another in random pairs.

"Xi, remember those crop circles outside of Pasadena?"

"Yes. The spinners?"

The spinner is a classic alien design. Usually they look like a propeller with three blades. Each of the blades is comprised of a series of stacked circles. That's what the particles in the gel remind me of, only they're orbiting one another, occasionally connecting in brief copulations.

"It's like the spinners, only some of them are linked together by a double helix."

"You're right," she says softly.

The particles are constantly dislodging from their partners, then reincorporating with others. I try to focus on just one of them, but it's like tracking a single ant in a massive swarm. Even Caleb stops his nervous pacing to watch. I notice he's no longer wringing his hands. We observe the white liquid dripping from Xi's fingers for what seems like an eternity, minor gods with a front row seat to creation.

Xi is the first to speak.

"Do you remember the verses on quintessence?" she asks us.

We all reverently chant, "My vehicle is matter. My awareness is light. Quintessence is the bridge between matter and light. I will submit to the Transit Light and follow its will in all things."

We repeat it several times, giving Caleb a chance to catch up. Then Xi dabs her finger in the hole where the substance is pooling. I notice that the aperture doesn't look natural. It's perfectly circular, like it's been drilled.

"Be careful," says Caleb. "Something down there has jaws like a snapping turtle and isn't afraid to use them."

"Bend down, Ohm," says Xi. I comply and she reaches forward to anoint my forehead with the strange fluid, as if she were purifying me with the blood of Christ. She uses her middle three fingers to trace the ridge between my eyebrows while reciting the mantra of quintessence. There is a brief moment where I recoil at having a potentially radioactive liquid smeared on my face, but then I smile at my squeamishness. She repeats the same process with Astra and Caleb. When it's Xi's turn, Astra does the honors by dipping her hand in Xi's palm. We stare at each other in the night, the glowing liquid painted on our foreheads like some tribal brand. It's as if we've given our vehicles over to something—conveyed ownership of ourselves. I don't know what inspired Xi, but it seems right. I close my eye and feel the Transit Frequency pulsing like a beacon in the night. Warmth begins to spread through my limbs, and for a few seconds I'm free from suffering.

I see it the moment I open my eye. It's hovering on the horizon, visible through the open space to the west. There's no need to say anything. My intense exhale is enough to catch everyone's attention. Soon all heads are turned.

"It's been almost a year." Astra's voice is choked with emotion.

"Is that it?" asks Caleb.

"That's it, brother," I say. "That's the real thing."

The Transit Light is bobbing up and down above the hills. Because I'm blinded on one side, I cannot gauge the distance. But then I remember you can never gauge the distance of the Transit Light. Sometimes it appears to be in front of the hills and at other times behind them. It could be just below the cloud line or closer to the outer atmosphere.

"You sure that's not a plane?" asks Caleb, his

glowing brow creasing in the darkness.

"Does that move like any plane you've ever seen?"

After a moment he says, "No, that's no plane. I don't know what it is, but it's no plane."

We all stand in prayerful concentration until the trance is shattered by a bloodcurdling scream. At first I think it's some kind of animal, then I sense the sentient rage. For some reason I'm reminded of a rabbit caught in the clutches of a giant owl, a prize carried aloft to be devoured in the coiled branches. I can picture the creature gripped in the predator's talons, emitting one long, terrible howl of outrage as it passes over the indifferent hills.

When the scream comes a second time, I realize it's not the cry of wounded prey, but a frustrated predator.

~

It's strange how people are so afraid of snakes and spiders when the animal you really have to worry about walks on two legs.

"I'm comin' to get you, motherfuckers!"

I quickly douse the light, hoping we haven't given away our position. There are three figures moving toward us from the other edge of the cemetery. The foremost yells with incoherent rage while the other two stumble in his wake. A woman's laughter trickles over the gravestones.

"You hear me, motherfuckers! This shit's gonna stop! You stinkin' motherfuckers!"

"Is he talking to us?" asks Xi, her eyes tracking the figures as they zigzag among the gravestones, pausing at the deputy's scorched corpse.

"They done burned him, Donnie," says a second male voice, tinged with drunken mirth. This is followed by another demonic howl from the leading shadow.

"Motherfuckers!"

I have never heard anything like it. It's as if the primal aggression circuit has been left wide open, totally overwhelming the guy's central nervous system. His awareness level is barely above that of a chimpanzee cannibalizing a member of a rival troop.

"Who's that?" I hiss. I realize there's nothing but the shadow of the hickory tree to obscure us.

"I'm afraid that's Donnie Dewberry," whispers Caleb. "Not the guy I would really want to run into out here if I had a choice. I'm guessing that's his old lady, Tammy. And that would be his cousin bringing up the rear. I think his name is Alan. Not a bad old boy on his own, but not real bright. Donnie isn't a real good influence on him."

"Who is he calling a *motherfucker*?"

"No one in particular. Donnie's the sort of guy that sees the whole world as a bunch of motherfuckers. It's kind of like his philosophy. Anyway, I figure you just found out who's been robbing these graves." As Caleb finishes his sentence, the lead figure drops to his knees at the charred patch, then howls at the moonless sky. This is followed by another string of profanities.

"The Transit Signal has scrambled his circuits," I observe. "He must have a high degree of sensitivity. Otherwise, he would never have found this place. Often times it's the broken vehicles that are the most sensitive."

"Yeah," says Caleb. "I don't suppose any of you brought a gun, did you?"

Our collective silence returns a deafening answer.

The lead figure suddenly pauses, and though I can't see him, I know his eyes are on us.

"Shit," says Astra. "The dome light."

I glance over my shoulder and notice the faint glow coming from the Subaru. No sooner have I turned around than the figures are advancing in our direction.

"Who the fuck is up there!?" shouts the voice. "You better have a goddamn good reason for being out here!" As I studied the approaching shadows I noticed the silhouette of a gun slung around the speaker's neck.

Before I can react, a spotlight is shining on my face.

"Well looky here, Donnie. I don't believe I know these folks. Maybe they're the ones that burned up old Deputy Gentry. I guess they're the sort that don't mind trespassing."

"We're trespassing too," says the girl, laughing.

"Shut the fuck up," replies the lead figure. I study the eyes glinting just above the spotlight. I recognize him with a sinking feeling in my chest. It's the man from the service station.

"I seen these sons-of-bitches," he says, glaring at me with such hate, it makes me sick. I've never spoken to this man, but he looks at me as if I've just run over his child. "Back at Rudy's. I knew they was up to no good." The light lingers on Xi for a moment. "Only I thought this one was a boy. Alan, these folks came all the way from California. How's that for dumb?"

"That's a long way to come for an ass-kicking," guffaws his sidekick.

"Hey, ain't that Caleb Starnes?" says the girl. "Whatcha doing out here, Caleb? I thought you'd done run off with the rest of them."

"No," says Caleb in a measured voice. "These folks just come out here to pay their respects to a friend of theirs."

A light plays across the half-dug grave. "Holy shit," says the lead figure. "I know who you motherfuckers are. You're the dumb shits that tried to kill themselves and hitch a ride on that spaceship. I see you done found Cody's grave. We was lookin' for it last night, but we had to settle for old Deputy Gentry instead. I always did have a grudge against that motherfucker."

"He's the one that arrested Donnie for disorderly conduct," says Tammy by way of explanation. "Hey, look at the big one, Donnie. He looks like Frankenstein."

I can feel the scrutiny on my face like the flame of a welding torch.

"Where did you all get that glow-in-the-dark paint? I want some," she complains. "Donnie, make them give me some of that paint."

The wild-eyed man ignores her. "We'll take a lot more out of their hides than paint before we're done. They got a lot to answer for. You can bet they're behind all of this crazy shit that's been going on around here."

"Look, Dewberry. These folks ain't your enemy. They know there's something wrong. They aim to put things straight by taking Cody out of here. Maybe it's not a bad idea just to let things be." Caleb's voice remains measured, reasonable.

"You know, I hadn't thought about burning the bodies the way you done the deputy," says Donnie, ignoring him. "Could be, that's not such a bad idea. There's something rotten under the soil around here. I can feel it in my guts. It all started when they brought that lousy faggot back here. It wasn't a lot at first, just a trickle. But then it got loud."

The man's face creases in pain, remembering the way the Transit Frequency had tormented him over the intervening months. He's one of the most dangerous types of humans there are. He understands that he's suffering, but cannot discern the cause. So he lashes out at everything around him.

"Look," I say, smiling. "We don't want any trouble, bro. We come in peace. All we want to do is just take our friend home. That's all."

I see the barrel of the weapon swing in my direction. I'm not an expert on firearms, but I know it's a medium caliber rifle with an extended magazine. The parts are not wood-colored like the guns I used to see when I was a kid, but all black. I doubt there's anything organic in the entire mechanism—nothing but metal and plastic. It seems to stare at me with black insect eyes.

"First thing, Frankenstein. I ain't your brother. And the second thing is you're a trespassing motherfucker. I don't know what the three of you stirred up out there in California, but you had no right to bring that shit back here. A lot of good people have been run out of their homes. I know for a fact it has something to do with this place." I see his eyes scanning the cemetery. "The dead are trying to chew their way out of the ground—driving everyone mad. I can hear them. They're just chomping away, day and night. Makes it so a body can't sleep. But that shit's about to stop. I take one look at the three of you, and it don't take a genius to figure out you've got something to do with it."

"You mean these are the folks that thought Cody was Jesus?" asks the second man, just now catching up. Caleb is correct. He isn't very smart.

"That kind of thinking ain't right," says the woman, now outraged. "That goes against the Bible."

"The Bible ain't shit," growls Donnie. "It's a bunch of trash written by goddamn Arabs."

"Now, I asked Pastor Bailey about that, and he says you're wrong. The Bible was written by white folks, just like us."

They go on like this for a while and I am struck by how little I really know about the world, having never ventured any further east than Barstow. In some ways, I'm just as provincial as these hill people. It's like I've encountered some remote, cannibal tribe in the forests of Borneo. Who needs science fiction when alien species exist just a two-day drive from home? Then I think about Quint growing up in a place like this and my body shudders.

This is what he came from.

"You want to drag one of them like we did old Medders' dog last night?" says the second man. "What about the black gal?"

"No. I got other plans for her. As a matter of fact, I got plans for all of them."

"Look," I say. "Quint may be sending out a signal that's affecting your judgment. Certain portions of your brain are over-activated right now. If you let us finish, we'll have him out of here and you'll never see us again."

Suddenly the man crosses the space between and I feel the barrel of the gun shoved under my chin.

"How do you like that, Frankenstein?" The man's breath smells like stale cigarettes. "If you don't shut the fuck up, ain't none of you going to be seen by no one ever again. Now you know how the folks around here have felt with that crazy buzzing in their ears. How does it feel to have a gun shoved in your face? Kind of sucks, don't it?"

I know there's going to be trouble the moment it bubbles from the depths of my guts. I try to stop it, but it's impossible. Suddenly I'm laughing. Of course I know what it feels like to have a gun shoved in my face. I've lived with a gun shoved in my face for most of my life. The question strikes me as absurd. I'm not even afraid. Not one little bit. I know it's a bad idea to laugh in the face of so much rage, but the entire situation suddenly strikes me as ludicrous.

The butt of the rifle strikes me across the face and I fall hard. I hear Astra yell, "Stop!" as she intercedes between me and the angry local. The blow stuns me for a moment. I have no doubt he's going to shoot me and Astra, yet even at this moment, I can't blame the guy. He's just following his programming. Getting angry at him would be like getting angry at a hungry bear for biting you. It's what they do. It's all they know.

My face stops him. The mask fell off when he

struck me.

"Damn, Frankenstein. You're totally fucked-up," laughs the second man.

"Yeah, Donnie. It looks like those aliens burned half his face off," says the girl. "Or maybe God punished him for believing in those UFOs."

I watch the man hesitate, his eyes peering down the length of the barrel. For just a split second there's a moment of recognition. I may not have a lot in common with this guy, but one thing we both understand is suffering. At our core, we both know what fuels the world—pain, pure and simple. It's not like we'll ever break bread together, though. The difference between us is that I'm looking for a way out of my vehicle. He identifies with his suffering so completely that he must inflict his inner pain on the rest of the world. All he can do is hurt the *motherfuckers.*

"All right! Enough of this horseshit! Y'all get in the hole! You bunch of glowing-assed motherfuckers! You're gonna keep digging, then we'll have ourselves a little bonfire of our own."

~

I sit with a cool soda can pressed against my swelling forehead while Xi and Caleb dig. My ears are still ringing from the blow. I no longer bother with the mosquitoes.

"I can't believe Quint grew up in a place like this," says Astra.

Donnie stands over the diggers, like some chain-gang boss.

"I'll tell you a story about your messiah," he says, turning to her. The upward lighting gives his face the appearance of surprise. "I went to school with him. He wasn't nothin'. In fact, he was less than nothin'. You talk like you're educated, but they must have filled your head with nothin' but shit. The Boatwrights was the poorest people around here, and that's sayin' something. He always smelled like rotten eggs because they didn't have no running water."

A part of me wants to tell him to shut up, but I sense truth in his words. It's like having an infidel narrate the story of your prophet. But that's the way it is. We don't have the luxury of a hundred years to create a new cover story. I can see that even Xi is paying attention.

"The teachers had a good bit of sport with him. Especially old Mrs. Mayo. Goddamn, she was a bitch."

"I remember her," intercedes his friend, now leaning against a tombstone, nursing a bottle. "She didn't like no one."

"I never did think much of her," adds the girl.

"I remember one day she drug him up to the front of the class. He kept falling asleep. She decides she gonna thrash him right there for a little wake-up call. So she goes to pull his pants down…She never done any of the rest of us that way, just him. That's just how low the Boatwrights was looked at. Well, there he is, wearing some girl's panties about two sizes too big for him. I think they was handed down from his older sister and man was them things dirty. I laughed until I puked when Mrs. Mayo tore into him with that old cane of hers. Poopy-Panties. That's what we called him. Poopy-Panties. There's your prophet. Lord and Savior Poopy-Panties."

"I didn't know he had a sister," I say. "You know what happened to her?"

"Who gives a shit," he replies, irritated. Clearly I missed the point of the story.

"I think she got a job taking care of old folks up north," says the girl.

"Man, you couldn't pay me enough to do that." The man with his back up against the tombstone is starting to slur his words. "Old people stink."

"At least she got out of here," says Astra through gritted teeth. I know it's a mistake the moment the words tumble out of her mouth.

Donnie Dewberry's eyes flash. "And just what's wrong with *here*? You got some place better to be? Don't come in here acting like the Queen of Sheba!" Without warning he fires three rounds though the engine block of the Subaru. The concussion leaves my ears ringing. "There, now you ain't going nowhere neither, bitch!"

"Shit, Donnie. You're gonna have the sheriff out here. You know I got a warrant." The girl's voice is plaintive.

"That sheriff ain't coming anywhere near this place," the man spits. He points the gun at Astra. "You best shut up, Sheba, or the next one's going between those pretty eyes of yours."

I don't get the impression he's going to shoot this time. He's enjoying himself too much. As I watch him gloat, I search inside myself for the crisis of faith that has plagued me over the past year. But instead, I find my resolve growing. You would think that hearing such degrading stories about Quint would cause me to lose what little belief I had, but it's quite the opposite. I wipe the sheen of sweat off my pasty skin, struggling against the suffocating humidity. As I sense the things tunneling under the earth or sailing through the night air on silent wings, I'm filled with awe for Quint. His faith was not born out of a desire to exploit or deceive. He never tried to force anyone to stay. He was trying to provide a pathway from the wrack of suffering we all share. And he had seen it. He had been shit out of the asshole of the world, I have no doubt of that. The true prophet wouldn't come from a place like Malibu. Only a testing ground like this could breed a visionary like Quint. The realization is sobering.

I take a moment to study Donnie Dewberry's companions. They're both a good bit younger than him. The girl is blonde with a dark blue streak in her hair. She's probably fashionable for the hills, but where we're from, she would get tagged as white trash all day long. She carries herself with an air of self-importance, still at that age when it's all about ego gratification. The man named Alan is getting drunker by the moment. There's nothing overtly cruel in his face. He's simply a follower. It strikes me that Donnie is somewhat similar to Quint in one respect. People have gravitated toward him. These two creatures have followed him to this remote cemetery, drawn to the beacon of hate that pulses inside him. But rather than looking for an alternative to the savagery of these hills as Quint did, this man personifies it. He's nothing more than an extension of the predatory hunger that drives the other living things in this place.

"I can't believe you would hook up with a bunch of losers like these, Caleb. Your daddy would sure be proud." His voice drips with sarcasm. "Did Caleb tell y'all anything about himself?"

Caleb keeps his eyes on the dirt, swinging the pick with just a little more force. I'm sorry for dragging him into all of this. I should have just left him alone. But he hasn't he tried to renounce us like most people would. That says something.

"Old Caleb here was gonna be a preacher like his daddy. Hell, he was a youth minister down at Brightwater Baptist. He even got himself a convert. What was her name, Caleb?"

The man is really enjoying himself now.

"It was Chelsea. Right? Remember how that went? Old Caleb here went to baptize her, only she come out of the water dead. His first convert and damned if he didn't kill her. She was alive when she went down, then dead when she come up. That ain't a real good track record."

"No one knew she had a heart condition," Caleb mutters.

"Caleb didn't do nothing after that. He just set up there in that trailer of his and moped. First goddamned baptism and he kills the bitch. How about that for the holy touch? Maybe you should fly off with your flying saucer buddies because it's sure as shit clear God wants no part of you."

The man's exposition is suddenly interrupted when Caleb jumps out of the hole. At first I think he has reached his limit, that he's attacking the man with the gun. But to my surprise, he clambers into the weeds, then turns to help Xi.

"Get out of there! Now!" He yells, yanking her up.

"What the hell do you two think you're doing?" Donnie barks.

Caleb ignores him and peers down into the darkness, his eyes fixed on the dirt. Xi is the first to notice his ankle. "I'm going to need a first aid kit," she informs Donnie.

I can see a trickle of blood dripping from his pant leg.

"There's something down there," says Caleb, his body tensed for flight.

"Like hell! You just can't swing a pick for shit. Alan, go check out that hole."

The drunk man leaning against the tombstone looks up blearily. "Why me?"

"Because once I determine beyond a doubt that

there ain't nothing in that hole, I'm gonna kick the shit out of this asshole. Now get up!" He prods the man's boot for emphasis.

Alan slowly crawls to the edge of the grave, now nearly four feet deep. He peers over the edge. "Donnie, there ain't nothing down here but…" His voice trails off. "What the hell is that?" He turns awkwardly so that his feet are hanging over the side.

"What is it?" asks Donnie, growing more irritable.

"I don't know. The dirt's moving. It must be a snake—or maybe a groundhog. I'll put a boot to its head, then we can have look at it."

As I watch the bizarre drama unfold, I'm reminded of the long chain of evolution that links us all—those ever-changing conditions that shape the fitness of each species. Caleb was right about this guy not being very intelligent. I wonder how many close calls he's survived in the past—all the times he cornered too fast on the brush-hog or leapt from a cliff into shallow water. This is one of those moments when his precarious genes will get put to the test. He lunges into the grave and begins stomping at the earth like it has offended him in some unforgivable way.

"There! How do you like that, you son-of-a-bitch?" he says for emphasis.

Then his tenor changes. When he begins screaming, I cringe. I've never heard a noise like it. There's something about our culture that likes to keep pain and death quiet. But there's nothing quiet those screams. Caleb had been too fast for it. But this man, his senses dulled, is not.

"Shitfire! Jesus! Donnie! It's burning my leg! It's burning my leg!" He leaps from the grave as if propelled by a catapult and begins leaping around the cemetery, his body convulsing in spasms of pain. He looks like a broken marionette on speed. I have just enough time to glimpse a tail wriggling from the bottom of his pant leg. For some reason, my mind returns to my childhood fish tank. I had this thing called a loach, it was kind of a cross between an eel and a catfish.

"Oh my god, help me, someone!" he screams. His voice is so high-pitched that, if I hadn't been watching him, I wouldn't have been able to discern if his cries were emanating from man or boy.

The girl moves to comfort him, but it's clear she doesn't want to touch him. Soon his limbs are jerking, as if something is electrocuting him. Spit flies from teeth that are cracking under the pressure of his bite.

"Do something, Donnie!" she shrieks.

For his part, the man with the gun can only stand and watch, his mouth hanging open. The thing is chewing its way up his inseam—right up the femoral artery, causing a gout of blood to discharge down his leg. Then his eyes widen until they are almost ejected from their sockets.

"Christ, Donnie," he manages to gasp through locked teeth. "It's burning its way through my asshole! It's burning inside of me."

Then I remember something. I turn to Astra and ask, "Do you recall the Rudra/Mahakala myth that Quint told us about?" But when I look over my shoulder, she's gone. I try to remember the story. There was something about a terrible demon named Rudra that stalked the world of the dead until the Buddha stormed from the heavens and enlightened him by penetrating his rectum. After this violation, Rudra was transformed into Mahakala, becoming the protector of the dharma. That's how it is with the Buddhists. They never imprison their demons like the Christians, but try to rehabilitate them.

"It's in my guts, Donnie! It's chewing up my guts!" The man is convulsing. His contortions are so violent, I'm surprised that his spine isn't severed. I am also equally surprised he's still conscious. A bloodstain quickly spreads out from his groin and the girl steps back, her hands plastered over her ears.

"Make him stop screaming! Make him stop!" she yells.

Then it happens. Donnie steps over to his friend and points the gun at him. There are three sharp cracks as the rounds slam into his chest, causing his body to bounce off the ground repeatedly. His blood consecrates the milkweed and briars that line the cemetery in a gory benediction.

Then everything is quiet for a moment. The man with the gun stands there, a slight tremor running through his body. The sounds of the katydids seem amplified in the momentary silence.

"You shot him," says the girl. "My god, why did you shoot him?"

"Shut the fuck up!" he barks.

"But you didn't have to kill him. What are you gonna tell his mama?"

The man hardens, then turns the gun on us. I sit cross-legged on the ground, awaiting the bullets like a beggar seeking alms. Caleb is sitting next to me while Xi applies pressure to his ankle with her shirt.

"You goddamned sons-of-bitches!" the man screams. "I'm gonna tell his mama that I shot the sorry motherfuckers that killed her baby!" With that, he slings the weapon down low, preparing to spray us from the hip.

I don't see Astra until she's right next to him. She simply appears like a holy Madonna, bringing her hand to the man's ear. Then Donnie's head is engulfed in flames. The thunderous boom echoes off the hillsides. He doesn't even twitch when he hits the ground. It's like magic. I honestly wonder if she's found some type of ray gun the aliens carelessly discarded in the cemetery—that's just how much fire erupts from her hand. But when I look a little closer, I see that it's a snub-nosed .357.

"And to Astra is given the fire of salvation!" I shout, my laughter momentarily drowning out the ringing in our ears.

~

Leave it to Xi to be the first one to extend aid to the people who, only moments before, were ready to kill her. "The signal can have an adverse effect on those who have not prepared their vehicles," she explains. Even now, she doesn't want to blame them for their actions. There isn't much she can do. Astra's round passed directly through our tormentor's temple. She was standing so close the flash from the gun barrel set his hair on fire. Donnie Dewberry will no longer terrorize the *motherfuckers* haunting his dreams. He lays on the ground, his head smoldering. His young friend presents a more complicated situation. When Xi palpates his chest, she detects movement inside the cavity. The thing is still burrowing.

"It's penetrated through his perineum and appears to be working its way up the spinal column toward the brain," she affirms.

"What is it?" I ask.

"A firm identification would require a surgical intervention that I am not prepared to undertake, but I would suggest it's some type of parasitic fluke."

"A grave fluke?" I say, testing the word. "I like that. It kind of makes me think about those maggots that greeted us at the entrance to the cemetery. Ever since we got here, I can't shake the feeling that the ground is writhing under our feet. There's no telling what's down there with Quint's awareness permeating the soil.

"Every other animal has cleared the area," says Caleb, testing the field dressing Xi placed on his ankle. "I think Xi's right. It looked like a mutated parasite. It probably dropped out of some possum's ass, then got caught in the signal. Can this Transit

Frequency create a monster like that?"

"Quint said that it kept reality in a constant state of flux when amplified," I explain. "It's entirely possible that it could impact morphology. It hits you at a cellular as well as a perceptual level. There certainly seems to be increased insect activity in the area. The cells in that thing's body are probably transducing the signal. I'm not sure why it's so aggressive, but you can bet there's a reason."

"Well, there ain't nothin' that surprises me anymore. By the way, that stuff Donnie said about me—about that girl I baptized. He was telling the truth. Most folks around here won't have nothin' to do with me because of that. It's not the type of thing I like to talk about."

"Don't sweat it, man. We've all got baggage. If you don't, you haven't lived. You don't need to tell us your life story, I know what it's like when words fail. People talk and talk, but sometimes there's nothing to be said. Lives are catastrophic gifts from our creator."

Caleb shakes his head, then stands slowly, testing his injured ankle. He studies the two bodies. "I thought you guys were pacifists."

"Whatever gave you that idea?" says Astra. She has the pistol stuffed in her waistband and the rifle slung over one shoulder. She reminds me of one of those badass BLA revolutionaries back in the seventies, the kind that scared white cops shitless. "Quint thought about stockpiling weapons at one point. Remember what they did to those people in Waco. It doesn't pay to buck the system in America. But we never got around to doing it; we figured the Transit Light would beat the feds to the punch."

"I didn't know you were packing," I say. "You set that guy's head on fire."

"You think I'm gonna come way out here naked? No fucking way. I know I'm going to die somewhere, but not in this godforsaken shithole if I can help it."

I know what she means. It's like some sort of primitive superstition with me as well. I would hate to die in these hills, as if they might trap my soul forever.

"Where did Tammy go?" asks Caleb. We all look around, but the girl is nowhere to be seen. "She might go to the law. I really don't want to be around when they get here. We're talking about a double homicide and those deputies aren't big on details, if you know what I mean. Throwing the whole bunch of us in prison is a lot simpler than doing some big investigation."

"You think there are more of those things down

there?" I ask, peering over the rim of the grave. Then something catches my eye. "Hey, man. They must have done this on the cheap. There's no vault. That's wood down there." My jaw is still swelling, but I no longer feel dazed by the blow from the rifle butt. Suddenly, my sense of purpose returns. We need to snatch Quint's body, then make a run for Malibu. They might get us eventually, but there's no point in making it easy on them. We just need to stay clear for a week, maybe two.

Slowly, I lower myself into the grave. The hole is aglow with the strange liquid. I glance around nervously, wondering if there might be more grave flukes waiting for me to turn my back. There's blowing your brains out and then there's getting devoured from the inside by a giant parasite. I prefer the former. Clearing the dirt away from the coffin, I see it's one of those old-fashioned toe pinchers. It's an interesting choice for Quint. Our style back in Malibu tended toward the futuristic, so I pictured him in a glowing tube or something. But as I think about it, the plain, pine box makes sense; he was always an acetic at heart.

I look up to find Xi handing me a crowbar and a rubber mallet. She's once again wearing the Ethereal Transit Society uniform with the emblem at her breast. Clearing some dirt away from the lid, I use the mallet to pound the crowbar into place, then prepare to pry with all my strength. While I'm not really thrilled about digging up a decaying body, it will be good to see Quint again, however ruined his visage. I keep my expectations low, especially since the coffin isn't pressure sealed. To my surprise, the lid gives way easily. I push it open, then stand aside so the lantern can reveal the bottom of the hole.

"Goddamnit!" says Astra. "Why does everything have to be so hard?"

"You got that right," I sigh, my chest deflating. There's nothing inside the box. We're staring at an empty grave. I lean against the side of the hole, clapping the dirt from my hands.

This time it's Caleb's turn to laugh. Then he tosses out more scripture.

"Trembling and bewildered, the women fled from the empty tomb, for they were sore afraid."

It's just our luck to have taken up with a preacher.

~

"He never had his body shipped. This whole thing has been a waste of time." Astra sits cross-legged on the grave marker, her chin resting on her hand.

Slowly, I run my fingers along the underside of the coffin lid, then find what I'm looking for. "No. He was here all right. We were beaten to the punch." I show them the scarred wood where someone recently pried it open. A like-minded soul popped the cork, then filled the hole back in. With the soil so fucked-up around here, there's no way to tell when the dirt was turned. That means those roots were not a year old, but maybe only days. I drop the lid back in place. Caleb and Xi help me out of the hole.

"You got any ideas?" asks Caleb.

"I don't know. It obviously wasn't one of these geniuses." I motion to the two dead men. "What about the cemetery keeper? He seemed to be tolerating the signal…barely. What do you know about him?"

As Caleb describes the man's sparse history, I find it difficult to listen. First of all, his voice is faltering and he has difficulty finishing sentences. The signal is really getting to him. Then I'm distracted by a searing pain in my ass. I reach back to massage the area, but recoil with singed fingertips. My phone drops to the ground, smoke pouring from the casing.

"Damn defective battery," I curse, then I see the vapor coming out of Astra's gym bag. All of our phones are cooked, the transduction elements fried beyond capacity. As I watch the plastic melt, I can actually hear the Transit Signal ringing in my head. It's almost as if the titanium plate is vibrating in sympathy. If we don't find the source soon, my head may be the next thing that catches on fire.

"Do not resist the signal. Allow it to pass through your vehicle," advises Xi, who rubs Caleb's shoulder. He's trembling. I can tell by his eyes that if the signal gets any stronger, he will go into shock. I look toward the caretaker's house. It's not that I want to go knocking on the door of a man with a flamethrower, but our vehicles are coming to the end of their endurance. The central nervous system can only take so much. I have no idea what time it is—probably early morning. The world around us is moving faster. Even the cadence of the katydids seems faster. I wonder if the very particles of the matter around me are starting to accelerate.

"Well, well, well," says Astra, standing. "Look who came back."

We turn and see that the girl has returned. She stands, shaking, her arms wrapped around her chest. I guess she doesn't want to face the deputies either. She avoids looking at her dead friends, staring at us instead with a mixture of hate and fear.

I rummage through my brain for her name. "Hey there, Tammy," I say carefully, as if speaking to an injured bird. "You doing OK?"

She locks eyes with me. For a moment I think she might lunge at me, but then I see the confusion in her eyes. When she speaks, her voice is weak and shaky.

"Do any of y'all know what that is?" she says, pointing over her shoulder.

We've all been so absorbed with Quint's grave, it hasn't occurred to me to check the sky. We walk out of the shade of the hickory so we can look toward the clearing in the west. I find my feet getting heavier with each step. Pinpricks of energy tickle my flesh.

"My God," says Astra. "It's beautiful."

All I can do is shake my head. It takes me a moment to realize that my mouth is hanging open.

"It ain't beautiful," says the girl spitefully. Then, in a more pathetic voice, "Can you make it go away? Please, can you make it go away?"

The Transit Light has never been this large before. It hangs on the western horizon like a counterfeit sun, only it burns with many colors. Greens, reds, and ambers mix together in strobing patterns. My guts start to seize up and I wonder if I am about to shit myself. It's still difficult to tell if the object is in front of or behind the terrestrial mountain layer below. In fact, I'm not sure if it's coming closer, or just getting larger in the sky, absorbing energy from some invisible source. I get the impression it's spinning at an incredibly high speed, like one of those super-dense neutron stars. Then I hear it. It's the Transit Tone—deep and resonant. Now the sound is overtly audible, vibrating the earth.

The Transit Light confirms its distance and discharges a massive surge of static with the earth. This manifests as a lightning bolt that surges toward the ground, striking a distant slope. I watch as a massive chunk of wooded hillside erupts in a fireball. For a long time, there's nothing but the hum of the signal and the increasingly frantic insects. I can see the glowing fire in the distance. Finally, a deep, resonant crack of thunder shakes the ground and the hair on my arm stands on end.

"I make it nine miles by the soundwave," says Caleb. "You folks ever seen it do anything like that before."

"No," is all I can say, a tear sliding down my cheek. Sobs threaten to burst from my body. I have been waiting for this moment for almost ten years, and all I can do is blubber like a baby.

"Can't you make it go away?" pleads the girl again.

"No," I say, regaining some measure of control. "It's coming. It's coming for real this time." Then I am struck by fear. "We're not ready! We need Quint to transduce the signal. We've got to find Quint."

"You guys know what to do, right? I mean you've been talking to this thing for years." Caleb glances at each of us for confirmation.

"Quint never made any guarantees. All he offered was a chance," says Xi. "You can either live your life in obscurity, working and procreating for nothing, or you can attempt to transcend your status as a material being. This is no church of fairy tales. Heaven isn't a birthright. Quint offered the possibility — the chance to become something more than you are. But that means solving the problem of transduction. Think of it as a final test."

Caleb's eyes widen with hesitation. He looks like a man in the throes of a fundamentalist hangover. I know what he's thinking.

Maybe I got carried away. Maybe I converted to the wrong god.

"If it makes you feel any better, I think this is a one-way ticket," says Astra, winking at him. "It's not going to stop. Yeah, this is a one-way ticket for everyone—all seven billion of us. The great recycling is at hand."

She checks the clip on the rifle then turns to the girl. "Honey, you can do whatever you want, but the fact is everything you know is about to change. No matter how far underground you burrow, it will find you. Your only chance is to stick with us."

"That ain't true," spits the girl. "That ain't gonna happen. Jesus won't allow it."

Astra laughs like an avenging Kali. "No, baby girl. It's on. If you are going to fuck with the gods, you better learn how to fly. And you better learn fast."

With this, she turns and begins picking her way toward the caretaker's house. I turn back and study the Transit Light one more time, trying to discern a pattern to the strobing flashes. I can't articulate its meaning on a conscious level, but I know it's saying something. My body senses it as predatory rage, but that isn't accurate. I know my brain is only capable of transcribing the signal into primitive feelings. Astra's right. This is a one-way ticket. It's coming.

The Transit Light is coming.

~

Xi turns the insignia in her hands.

"Are you sure it's Quint's?" I ask, though I know it's an asinine question the moment it leaves my lips. What would a dirt-encrusted ET symbol be doing in front of the caretaker's house?

She strokes the insignia lovingly, one finger tracing a small imperfection in the metal. The night has sickened during the twenty minutes it took to pick our way through the woods. The sky overhead is churning like a stomach about to eject its contents. The haze has given way to a series of swirls, the clouds hanging down in nauseating fingers. Even the katydids have been silenced. They worked themselves into a frenzy, leaving their singing mechanisms frayed. Now they hang from the tree limbs, paralyzed like rotting fruit.

An air current almost lifts me off my feet. "It's getting a little sporty out here," I laugh. We try to ignore Tammy's praying, which comes in steady counterpoint to the rising wind. She looks over her shoulder through the trees, as if some bloodthirsty deity is pursuing her.

In a way, she's right. But her prayers aren't going to help.

"Old Samson seemed a mite twitchy," says Caleb, his body still shivering. "You want me to try and talk him out?"

"No thanks, man," I say. "I'll do the honors. I've had so many guns pointed at me tonight, I'm kind of getting used to it. Astra will cover me."

There's no point in messing around. We can no longer see the Transit Light due to the trees, but I can feel its hunger. It's come to feed. The time for subtlety is over. Before I reach the door, Astra takes me by the arm, bringing her lips close to my ear.

"Is this what he showed you? The night you shot yourself. Is this what Quint wanted you to know?"

"Yes. At least it's the beginning. I think even he was having second thoughts. And it's going to get a lot worse."

As I approach the door, Astra takes up a position to my right. The others cluster a few yards behind me. I knock once. After a few seconds of silence, I call out. "Mr. Brody? We've come for Quint! We know you've got him."

The door opens abruptly and I'm face to face with the old man, his nostrils pulsating. He doesn't have a flamethrower this time, but a pump-action shotgun. His eyes play across my deformed features and his nose wrinkles in disgust.

"I knew you people were trouble from the moment I saw you."

"We've got nothing to do with this." I wonder if I

really believe my own words. "But we're trying to help. We need to find Quint."

He looks over my shoulder at the others huddled in the wind. I watch his finger tighten around the trigger. He can't see Astra in the shadows to his right, ready to spray the doorway with bullets at the slightest provocation.

"I don't deserve this," he says, shaking his head. "I've led a good life. At least, I haven't led a bad one. Folks around here don't deserve none of this."

"It's got nothing to do with deserving anything, Mr. Brody. This isn't a judgment. That thing out there doesn't care what kind of life you've led, but it wants something. It will tear these hills to pieces to get it."

I'm dimly aware that the Transit Signal is changing pitch. It almost sounds like a hog sucking at the earth. My ears begin to pop. Then there's that terrible cracking sound. The old man suddenly lowers the shotgun, his eyes fixing on something just over my shoulder.

It isn't the Transit Signal that's making the noise.

"Y'all best come inside. You'll want to huddle along the east wall. I've got it reinforced."

His sudden change in demeanor confuses me until I glance over my shoulder and see trees being shredded in the distance. It's a tornado, churning in the darkness like some type of blind, rabid beast. Suddenly there is no more arguing. We pile into the house. The man doesn't even complain when he sees Astra come around the corner with the rifle. Now he's just a decent human, saving strangers from an oncoming storm.

"They always come at night around here," is all he has time to say once we're all sitting alongside a wall just below ground level. It's decorated with a homey rose pattern. This man must have been married at one time. I wonder how long he's been alone. It reminds me of my own isolation before I found ET. That kind of loneliness does have one advantage—it prepares you for your own death.

I see the tempest through a side window, passing in the night. It's missing the house by about fifty yards. The trees aren't so much toppled as twisted out of the ground. Limbs churn in the darkness along with sheet metal from an abandoned chicken coop. As the cyclone sweeps across the hillside, it seems to lift off the ground for a moment, sparing the valley its rage so that it can deliver its wrath to the adjacent hilltop.

"Make it stop! Make it stop!" repeats the girl. It's not the tornado that disturbs her. Once it passes, the

Transit Signal's volume seems redoubled.

"I knew there was going to be problems the day I buried that old boy," says the caretaker, sitting down in an upholstered rocking chair with the weight of the world on his face. "The ground just wouldn't act right. Kept trying to suck down the backhoe. I stopped going back there to tend him. I didn't like the way my toes vibrated when I walked over his grave."

"You've got to take us to him. I'm not telling you we can stop what's happening—some things are already written. But it's not going to do any good to hide him."

There is a long pause after my words.

"I burned him—every bit of him. Right there, out yonder."

"Take us to him."

"I tell you, I burned that old boy."

"Just show us."

Finally, the old man stands shakily and walks to the door, pointing to a small cleared patch behind his house.

"You see that metal building right there? That's my welding shop. That's where I done it. Dug him up four days ago after things started getting really bad. Couldn't think of nothin' else to do. I doused his carcass, then put the torch to him."

I thank the man and stride into the night, but Xi lingers at his side for a moment.

"You could come with us," she suggests. "This is a journey that's open to everyone."

The man turns his milky eyes in her direction. "I'm tired," he says by way of reply. "It's all in God's hands now."

~

The welding shack is nothing but four slabs of corrugated sheet metal driven into the ground with a tin roof overhead. It's not really much of a church to house the remains of a saint. The gravel floor is clumped with axle grease and motor oil. The room reeks of combustibles. At the far end I see the burned patch. We gather around the remains of our teacher. He is nothing more than a cluster of charred bones.

Without thinking, the four of us join hands.

"Just as I fear the sunrise," I say, taking the lead this time.

"I will not fear death," Xi and Astra answer.

"Just as I do not fear the passing seasons."

"I will not fear the infirmity of my vehicle."

"For my body is a transient container."

"And my awareness will live forever as cosmic

energy."

I'm aware that the night outside is becoming brighter. The Transit Light is drawing nearer, casting shadows through the tree limbs. The metal roof is vibrating.

"Didn't he tell you what to do?" asks Caleb, his eyes fading in and out of focus.

"No," says Astra softly. "I don't think even he knew what to do. You just prepare your awareness, and hope you know what's required when the time comes."

"I don't mean to sound ungrateful, but that doesn't really sound like much of a plan."

I get down on my knees, examining the broken remains of Quint's skull. Xi sits beside me as Astra watches over my shoulder.

"The right side?" I ask, peering closely.

"That's correct," Astra says. "Right next to his ear. It was about the size of a marble."

Xi looks at each of us quizzically, falling back into that Scottish dialect. "Why, whatever are you talking about, Ohm?"

"He's looking for the implant," says Astra. "Quint might not have shown it to you. He only showed it to a few people. Ohm and I may have been the only ones." Her voice is conciliatory—

comforting. She doesn't want Xi to feel excluded.

My fingers sort through the debris on the floor. First I pick up and examine a large bolt covered in black tar and cooked human fat. I toss it away, cursing. Then I find what I'm looking for. It's considerably larger than a marble. I hold it up to the lamp light. It's multicolored and conical in shape, at least an inch long. The colors seem to blend one into the other. Inside there are swirls. It's the spinners— just like the shapes in the grave gel. The thing warms my palm. Even as I examine it, I can't determine how it was manufactured. It seems to transcend the categories of technology I'm familiar with. In fact, I wonder if it was even manufactured at all, so organic are the swirling images.

"How would you like to have that pressing into your brain all day long?" I ask the others.

"Poor Quint," says Astra. "To have endured so much pain."

The thing vibrates in my palm. I hold it up to my good ear and realize it's sending out its own signal. I press it against the plate in my head, allowing it to resonate with the titanium. Astra asks me what I'm doing, but I'm too focused to answer for a few seconds. There's a problem with the implant. It doesn't match the Transit Signal.

Why doesn't it match?

I wonder if it was damaged in the fire, but, on closer examination, it looks unscathed.

I hand the implant to Astra, who allows Xi to inspect it as well. I stare at the bits of charred skull. Quint's teeth are scattered on the ground like burnt popcorn. The answer is there. It has to be. I feel something building inside of me. We're so close. But I can't understand why the implant's signal doesn't match the light outside—the one that's growing nearer—causing the earth to quiver like a beaten dog.

"Y'all better do something fast," says the girl, shivering in the doorway. "That thing is coming into the valley below."

"How do we use it?" asks Xi, her fingers touching the surface of the implant. "It's almost like it's trying to harmonize."

That's when it hits me. "That's it! The mantra of light…Quint always told us to *submit* to the transit signal. That was wrong. You don't tune your body to it. You harmonize with it. We were just imitating its signal. Our organic vehicles have totally different signatures. We were trying to build a bridge over a river by starting on the wrong side. We need to build our own foundation first."

I see the realization dawning on the faces of Xi and Astra. Then the full weight of it hits me. "Poor Quint. He walked around with that thing in his head, fighting against it day and night. No wonder the tuning sessions were so painful for him. He was battling against the implant rather than harnessing its power. It's not designed to resonate with the Transit Light, but to challenge it. That's how we can make the transition."

Astra turns the thing in her hand. "I see the truth of it," she concedes. Then she passes it back to me. "Here."

"No," I say. "You were the first. You were always closest to him. You take it. You'll know what to do when the time comes."

~

My knees weaken as I behold the Transit Light in its full glory. It took us twice as long to traverse the pathway back to the clearing, picking our way through the twisted brush and debris left in the wake of the tornado. Now the Transit Light is much larger than the sun, hovering only a couple of miles from our position. There's another discharge of static, this time toward the sky. At first I can't tell what it connects with, but then I see the burning debris falling earthward. It's a passenger jet, flying at high altitude. Maybe it had been on its way to Denver or Los Angeles. The people on board never knew what hit them. One minute they were craning their necks to behold the fires of creation below, then they were gone. A second charge connects with a neighboring hill. Not only do the trees burst into flame, but I can see the slope give way in a massive landslide.

The girl is screaming. I sense Caleb behind me, sticking close to the three of us as if his salvation depended on it. I've spent much of my adult life seeking the Transit Light, trying to coax it to earth. But now that it's here, I feel like a terrified animal.

"The energy is still too unstable," says Xi. "Our vehicles with be obliterated along with our awareness. We need to find a way to activate the implant."

Astra turns it in her hand. "One of us needs to connect to it."

Here we're at a loss. It's tragic to come this far, only to fail. I sense that once the implant is fully activated, we will only get one shot at the transition.

Something tugs at my leg. I look down and see the girl, Tammy. Her hair is plastered to her forehead from the sweat. Despite being early morning, it must be a hundred degrees on the hillside. She points toward the cemetery, her mouth trying to form words. I see the two bodies where we left them, their skulls picked clean of flesh. The grave fluke, now gorged on meat, is coiled amid the scattered bones. There is a great puddle of the quintessence fluid on the ground around it, as if the thing has transmuted the man's flesh into the strange substance with which Xi anointed us. The grave fluke's head bobs this way and that, almost mocking us in the glare of the Transit Light. There is another static discharge in the distance. Soon the hillside is obscured in smoke, our lungs filling with the smell of burning timber. If we don't burn to death, one of those static discharges will atomize us.

"The eye is the lamp of the body," intones Caleb. At first I dismiss the words as a random utterance from a fallen preacher, but then it clicks. The others see it as well. As we stand, each of us on the precipice of oblivion, there is no need for words. There is only the unspoken covenant that the rites must be performed regardless of the cost. Astra discards her weapons and holds the transplant up to the light. I feel Caleb's arms moving under my shoulders, securing me in a full nelson. Xi removes a scalpel from the first aid kit at her waist.

My mind goes back to that motel room in Van

Nuys. I remember the ugly duvet and the benign decorations. I remember the clock ticking away the seconds of a life that seemed like it would never end. I couldn't stand being in my vehicle for one more second. That's what I was thinking the moment the bullet tore through my skull. There was no way to know that I was simply preparing the way, like a prophet in the wilderness.

I am the vehicle of transmission.

The hum of the Transit Light is almost drowned out by my screams. I'm surprised by Caleb's strength. He grips my hair with his hands, helping to keep my head still. Slowly Xi cuts through the scar tissue on my ruined eye socket, just in front of the titanium plate. I try to let the pain pass through me, but I find that the best thing to do is scream it out of my body.

But I never once ask them to stop.

There's the steady chop of an approaching helicopter. Then I hear the crackle of another static discharge and the sound stops.

When the bloody hole is open, Astra inserts the implant through the socket. She pushes slowly, as if inserting a suppository. I feel a strange pressure inside my skull, and then the pain is gone. Caleb releases me and I fall to my knees, panting. It took everything I had to endure the crude surgery, but I can feel the implant integrating with my central nervous system. Its signature frequency awakens the cells inside of my body and, suddenly, for the first time in my life, I feel alive. I immediately see Quint's mistake. How can you fight against a thing inside your brain? The pitch is higher than the Transit Frequency, but just inside the range of my vocal cords. I begin to hum it, ignoring the taste of blood inside my mouth. The frequency passes to the titanium plate. It too, begins to vibrate like a resonance panel.

I'm dimly aware of Astra's voice.

"Caleb, it's time for us to name your awareness. This is not the name of your vehicle, but the name of the being that struggles for freedom inside you. Your name is Telos, for you are the one who comes at the end. You are the one who was here to greet us when we came to fulfill our purpose."

"Thank you, Astra."

"Welcome," says Xi, embracing him. Then she places a hand on my shoulder. "I am sorry I injured your vehicle, Ohm."

I rise to my feet, the new frequency vibrating off the plate in my skull. The others find the pitch easily. Almost at once the Transit Light's random charges of energy cease. Now it hovers in front of us, completely stable. It continues sending the powerful signal that jangles your guts, but our tiny voices reach out to greet it like discarded children. Then as the others continue to harmonize, I begin a new mantra.

"My vehicle is matter. My awareness is light. Quintessence is the bridge between matter and light. I will *harmonize* with the Transit Light and *create a new world*." Quint could never get past this wretched place—the place that spawned him. It was a place of angry gods that drank the blood of sinners. Your only reward for a lifetime of obedience was pain. But something about this dark soil made him the gateway. Perhaps his pain tore the veil of reality. And now we would have the opportunity to step through. I wish he was here with us, but at least he left us with the tools to find the level beyond human. He couldn't lead us to the Promised Land, but he got us close enough.

As I study the undulating colors of the Transit Light, I think about the day Quint named us. There was never any ceremony. He would just inform you when the time was right. You might be doing the dishes or some other mundane chore, and he would whisper in your ear. Astra is the fire of creation. Xi embodies the simplicity of the acetic life. Telos, the fulfillment of purpose. And Ohm, the electrical resistance between two points. The beauty of it astounds me.

"You sick bastards are going to pay!" I'm dimly aware of the woman confronting us with the rifle. This time there's no hesitation. She pulls the trigger. But the weapon doesn't work. At first I wonder if the Transit Light has disabled it, but then I perceive the ammunition clip at our feet. Telos has emptied the weapons. That was fortunate.

I feel my body being accessed by the harmonizing signals. The transduction of my cells allows me to see the world as it is, a series of frequencies that hold matter together. The harmonics are reading each of us, parsing our awareness from the matter that we will soon leave behind. As I reach out, I can feel the frequency of every object around me, the code that maintains its molecular stability. My three companions are different from the surrounding matter. I can perceive them as pools of light increasing with intensity as each second passes. We are making the transition.

The girl shrieks with rage, then throws the gun to the ground, her hands balled into fists. There's a brief moment when my awareness touches the grave fluke and I understand its purpose. It's not a transduction element, but a converter. By devouring the human flesh, it has decoded our collective memory in its bloated coils. It writhes like the serpent in the pit, ready to fuel our journey to the stars. That touch from my awareness is all it takes. The creature explodes and we gasp as a series of glowing particles shoot into the air.

The spinners hover, their orbed blades rotating around the double-helix structures, defying the pull of gravity. The quintessence fluid was only the larval stage. Now they are fully formed. They dodge about the hillside like sprites, testing their new manifestation before beginning the harvest.

"It's time for the recycling," says Astra, and we each move inside ourselves, feeling our very matter being converted into pure awareness—preparing for the great journey that awaits us. One of the spinning particles darts toward the girl's head, burning a hole in that vacant flesh that once housed the third eye. She screams as her central nervous system is reduced to ash.

When her head explodes, thousands more of the tiny particles shoot into the sky, then dart off in all directions, scavenging the countryside at the speed of light. Somewhere in the distance I am dimly aware of the caretaker's screams as he too is taken. I wonder if those who are harvested will follow us into the Transit Light, but then I realize this is impossible. They will serve as fuel. Nor will we find our colleagues lost in Quint's premature launch.

The transition is imperceptible. One moment I am on earth, and the next my awareness enters the realm of light. It just happens. Then it's just the four of us inhabiting eternal space, feeling the energy around us getting stronger by the moment. Swimming in that cosmic sea, I play with the frequencies, realizing that I now have the ability to shape energy into matter—to create new, limitless forms. This place was not built. It's a natural phenomenon present at the first moment the universe was born. It's the great harvester of awareness, wielding its scythe with unflinching precision.

Behind us, the world is being consumed. People are waking up to a reality of dancing orbs that burn through their skulls and take everything that they ever were, sending them plunging into darkness. I allow my awareness to touch the surface of the planet and I can feel each one being snuffed out.

The boy is having a bad dream.

The utility worker is trying to restore power.

The woman is getting ready for work.

A mother is frustrated, dressing her child.

The child is alarmed when its mother starts screaming and clawing at her forehead.

I can feel the last thoughts of each one. At first, they come by the dozens—then by the thousands. Soon they are coming in at a rate of millions per second. I shouldn't have the ability to compute numbers that high, but I can. Not one of them is missed. I search my awareness for some sense of grief at such a massacre. There is none. The capacity for sorrow was discarded with my human vehicle. I wonder for a moment if the cycle will stop before they're all dead, but I know it won't. It will keep going until the billions have been reaped. Only then will the spinners return to feed the Transit Light.

A silent planet. Billions of corpses bearing the wound of the third eye.

That's when we will leave. Together, the four of us will push away from the planet like a ship departing harbor. Our discarded vehicles will be there on that hillside to greet sunrise, food for the worms. But we no longer need them. We will drift through the great abyss, powered by the pain of those who have been sacrificed to make the voyage possible.

Be sure about one thing. We are neither saints nor sinners. We are simply the orphaned apostles of the oncoming light.

About the Author

Thomas Vaughn is a fiction writer whose work encompasses dark magical realism. He is a byproduct of the debris field of rural Arkansas, a place he calls the archive of pain. When he is not writing fiction he poses a college professor whose research focuses on apocalyptic rhetoric and doomsday cults. He views the writing of fiction as integral to the struggle for higher awareness. Feel free to visit him at brokentransmitter.com.

About the Artist

Forensics and Flowers, created by Viki Lester is a small business creating illustration and goods with a dose of positivity, a splash of darkness and a sprinkle of magic.

www.forensicsandflowers.com

www.instagram.com/forensicsandflowers

# BAD DREAM ENTERTAINMENT

Dark Stories for Dark Minds

www.BadDreamEntertainment.com

www.Facebook.com/BadDreamEntertainment

www.Twitter.com/BadDreamPub

9 780099 603819 5